Homecoming Heart

Hearts of Three Rivers #2

AMITY LASSITER

For my parents, who have always supported whatever crazy adventure I've chosen to go on—including this one.

Hearts of Three Rivers

Runaway Heart

Homecoming Heart

ACKNOWLEDGMENTS

Thanks to Faye and Nikki for their critiques, my enormous base of beta readers who feed my ego... er... keep me humble.

To Sarah of SL Barrel Horses who answered my questions about training and prepping.

Many, many, many thanks go out to my editor, Keriann, who spent hours on the phone with me to help me figure out the inner workings of Noah Baylor.

Of course, as with anything I write, I have relied on and am so grateful for the support and patience of my family; my mother and father, my sister Shay, and Mr. Lassiter.

PROLOGUE

TWO YEARS AGO

HER COUNTRY MUSIC ring tone jerked Emma Pierce out of her peaceful slumber. Before she even rolled over, she knew who was on the other end of the line. She wiped her hands over her eyes, attempting to dissuade the sleep clinging desperately to her eyelids. She'd been up late packing and her body protested anything less than eight solid hours of sleep these days. There had been times when she hadn't hit her bed until this hour, but they'd become extinct in the last couple of years.

Groping in the dark, she flicked on the bedside lamp and picked up her cell phone. 3 am. There was no sense ignoring the call. He would call back until she picked up. She pinched the bridge of her nose as she put the phone to her ear.

"Hey." She tried her best not to sound like she felt.

"He's here again."

Through her grogginess, she laughed. "You and I both know there'd be no other reason for you to call me in the middle of the night, Banks."

Sheriff Banks Montgomery chuckled on the other end of the line, but he sounded as tired as she felt. "I'm sorry. You know he won't let me call his brothers."

"I know." Emma sat up, swinging her legs over the edge of the bed.

"You could just leave him, Emma. You should. He only makes me call you because he knows you'll come and get him."

She groaned, easing her bare feet onto the cold floor of her bedroom, keeping her voice quiet. "I'll do it one more time."

After Friday, he'll have to find someone else, she thought as she balanced her phone between her cheek and shoulder and ungracefully tried to pull on the crumpled pair of sweat pants she'd discarded on the floor just a few hours before when she'd fallen into bed.

"You're an angel, Emma Pierce."

"Sure am. See you in ten." She sighed and hung up the phone, sliding it into her pocket. She turned the tattered high school hoodie she'd left on the foot of her bed right side out and tugged it on, staggering toward the bathroom.

Flipping on the light, she squinted in its harshness at herself in the mirror, and then dragged her thick mess of dirty blonde hair into the best semblance of a ponytail she could muster. Moving to the small linen cupboard, she pulled out a clean washcloth, drenched it in cold water, and pressed it to her tired eyes.

These calls came at least once a month, and had for the last year. At first, she'd felt panic every time she saw the sheriff's phone number turn up on her phone. Now, she felt resignation.

Since the accident a year ago, she'd watched her closest friend and neighbor slowly deteriorate. Time was meant to soothe all wounds but instead of healing, Noah was doing more hurting these days than he had in the beginning, and it was starting to spread to those around him.

Stifling a yawn, she slipped out of her room and crept down the stairs. She grabbed her keys and stepped out into the night. It was only late summer but the temperatures had started to drop overnight and combined with the lack of sleep, it made her teeth chatter. She closed the door of her car quietly and turned the key in the ignition, immediately blasting the heat to try and get her blood circulating. After a second thought, she cracked the driver's side window so the fresh air would keep her awake, and then idled her car quietly out of her parents' driveway.

Banks was right. She should leave him there. A lifetime of friendship and a heart that couldn't quite make up its mind whether it wanted to jeopardize that friendship in search of something stronger got her out of her bed every single time.

Once he sobered up, he would apologize and things would go back to normal. Truth be told, she picked him up from the drunk tank as much for his family as for him. They'd suffered enough in the last year; between the accident, and much more recently, Sunny's cancer, they had enough on their plate. She was doing the neighborly thing, she told herself, as she turned up the radio and headed down the road toward the sheriff's office.

~

Noah Baylor sat with his elbows on his knees and his pounding head hanging. The fluorescent lights in the sheriff's office weren't helping anything, either.

Banks Montgomery sat outside of the holding cell, his arms crossed over his chest. Noah might have been three sheets to the wind but he could feel anger radiating off his old friend.

Jimmy Sullivan *had* been asking for it. He'd been talking some bullshit about Finn and Sunny and what a shitty husband Finn was for dragging a sick girl around the rodeo circuit. At the time, Noah never felt anything quite as satisfying as the crack of Jimmy's nose under his fist. People at the bar even let out a cheer when the asshole bit the dust. Hell, if Banks hadn't been wearing that sheriff's badge, *he* probably would have cheered, too.

Headlights flashed through the office window and made a trek across the opposite wall as they heard a car pull in, and Noah looked up. Banks rose and looked out, shaking his head.

"You're lucky she answers her phone every time."

"She's a good friend." Noah rose to his feet

and wrapped his fingers around the bars of the cell anxiously. Emma. His savior. Suddenly, he needed to see her, perhaps more than anything he'd needed in his life. She'd be gone soon and just the thought made his pulse race with panic.

"And you're a goddamn liar." Noah watched Banks pull out the outdated paper ledger they used to keep track of comings and goings and knew Emma's name was in there too many times.

Resisting the urge to tell Banks where to go, Noah released the bars and stepped back. He heard the door in the hall close and soon, Emma appeared. He let out a long breath and his heart rate started to slow.

She looked exhausted. Her dark blonde hair was piled on top of her head in some kind of attempt at a ponytail, and she'd covered her lush curves in baggy, tattered sweats. Large dark circles had formed under her bleary eyes. In that moment, she was the most beautiful thing he'd ever seen. And he felt like a rat bastard.

"Hey Emma."

"Hey Banks." She let out a sigh and looked over her shoulder at Noah, then focused her attention on signing the ledger. "Jimmy Sullivan again, eh?"

She didn't look up from her writing. Noah let out a deflated breath. Now, seeing how tired she was, how disappointed she looked, it hardly seemed worth it to have punched Sullivan. He should have called his brothers, his parents – anybody but her. She was the only one who wouldn't leave him there all night, and he'd taken advantage of that fact.

When he didn't reply, she shook her head. "Thought so."

Noah cursed silently as he watched Banks cross the room and unlock the cell, letting him out into the office.

"Go straight..."

"Yeah, yeah, go straight home. Don't get into any more trouble." Noah cut the sheriff off. He'd heard this lecture a dozen times.

"Jesus, Noah. I'm just trying to look out for you."

Emma stepped into Noah's line of view, blocking out Banks. She wrapped her hands around his forearms and tipped her head up, making eye contact that said *'Knock it off.'* and pulled him away from the other man.

"Straight home," she promised. "He won't be back here tonight."

Noah slipped Emma under his arm and tugged her soft, warm body to his side. She rolled her eyes at him but used the position to her advantage, steering him out of the office and to her car. He eyed the back seat full of boxes. It hit him in the gut like a fist.

"Getting a head start on the packing?"

He didn't know if the job in Denver was worth going for, but she'd always talked about leaving Three Rivers behind. Fantasized about it, even. She had been such a permanent and comfortable fixture in his life; he'd never imagined she would actually leave him. Panic seized the pit of his stomach again and he felt like retching.

"I leave in three days." She muttered, gesturing for him to get into the car. She slid behind the driver's wheel.

"Can't wait to leave me." He tried to tease, but it came out flat – he wasn't sure if it was because of the booze or the hard ache right under his sternum when he thought about a tomorrow that wouldn't include her face.

Her silence told him the answer. *Christ, what am I doing?*

~

Emma gripped the steering wheel and stared straight ahead. She could feel tears prickling behind her eyelids and she swore at herself. She was just tired, that was all. Was the job at the barrel racing outfit in Denver worth leaving everything she'd ever known? She glanced at her dashboard clock and at Noah slumped in the passenger seat and her resolve rose stronger. *Oh hell yes.*

She turned the key in the ignition and the drive to the Baylor ranch was wordless. Thirty seconds in, Emma turned on the radio in an attempt to ease the uncomfortable silence. They'd been friends for twenty three years, and silence was sparse between them, especially one that left so many unsaid words echoing around them.

As he always requested, she dimmed the car lights and pulled into the drive as quietly as she could. It was a farce; his family knew he'd gone to town after chores, they just had bigger fish to fry than worrying about the son who, although he was making stupid, irresponsible choices, was still alive. He was, after all, an adult.

Not for the first time, she wished they could rewind. They'd been friends nearly their whole lives, but that summer a year ago had been a turning point. They'd never put a word to it, but he hadn't had a girlfriend in months and they were inseparable...until that day they'd come home to find Banks standing in the yard with his hat in his hands. The accident that had claimed the youngest Baylor brother, Gavin, and his wife, June, and left their son, Gage, an orphan had rocked his family. Eight months later, his oldest brother, Finn, had lost his wife, Sunny, to aggressive cancer. For a year now, the Baylors, a family she considered her own, had been scrambling to find a foothold, each one grieving in their own way. Noah just happened to find his in the bottom of a bottle of whiskey, and avoided grieving at all.

She turned and shifted the car into park. Instead of climbing out like he normally did, Noah looked over at her with an anguished expression. She drew a breath. Emotional Noah sometimes came out to play when he was drinking, but this was different. He reached across the space between them and put his hand over hers on the gear shifter.

"Don't go." His words were choked.

It could have been feelings or it could have been the alcohol and she wouldn't have known any different anymore. She'd tried, for a year, to bring him back to the point he'd been at before the accident, but there was no amount of love or compassion that could do it, and she couldn't let herself get jerked around this way anymore.

Still, Emma's stomach did a somersault. She tried to laugh it off, sliding her hand out from under his.

"Noah, we *talked* about this," she said. Granted, he had been sober at the time. "This might be my only chance to get out of here. Denver's only a couple hours away. You can come and visit any time."

"I won't," he said, and she didn't know if it was defiance or disappointment she heard in his voice. "I don't know what I'll do here without you."

He was getting sloppy, and she could hear tears in his voice. In their lifetime of friendship, she'd only seen him cry when they'd gotten the news of Gavin's accident. Even at the funeral, he hadn't shed a tear. As they'd gathered around Sunny's bedside and watched her deteriorate until the cancer ate every part of her body, Noah had held strong. And here he was, fixing to blubber like a baby because she was moving a couple of hours away.

She stared across the space between them, her lips pursed. If he had asked her to stay a year ago, six months ago, even, with his warm hands on hers and the emotion she heard clogging his voice, she might have given up the idea of running as far and fast from Three Rivers as she could get. But the last year had been bad. And she loved Noah too much to say no when he needed a shoulder to cry on, or to just let the phone ring when Banks called her to pick him up from the sheriff's office. She was exhausted, and leaving was an easy out. And now she'd made her plans; he'd had months to ask her to stay.

In another life, this could have played out differently. He might not have even been at the bar, but safe in bed. With her. But this was *this* life – a world where she'd watched him pick fights and women she couldn't hold a candle to physically, a world where she was reminded that someone like Noah couldn't be attracted to someone like her. Even when he was drunk.

"I love you..."

She held up her hand to stop him and he sat back like she'd slapped him. This was a road they couldn't go down. Not tonight.

"Don't, Noah. You're drunk. Go inside. Sleep it off. We'll talk about it tomorrow."

But she knew they wouldn't as she watched him climb grudgingly out of the car and stagger toward the house. She would take the coward's way out, finish packing, and hide in her childhood bedroom at her parents' place next door until it was time to leave. She couldn't look in her rear view mirror as she drove away from the Baylor ranch.

ONE

Welcome to Three Rivers!
Come on in and stay a while!

EMMA TIGHTENED HER grip on the steering wheel as she navigated her sensible economy car past the freshly repainted sign that had always been a beacon telling her home was just around the corner. For most of her childhood, it had been a comfort as they pulled into the town limits returning from rodeos or shopping trips. It was the end of the trail, five minutes to her family's ranch and she could unload her horse and her bags and collapse into her familiar bed after an exhausting weekend.

Seeing it now, she wasn't sure how to feel about it. Her heartbeat ricocheted all the way down to the pit of her stomach as she signaled left and turned off the road toward her family's ranch.

A quarter of a mile down, she passed the

Baylor ranch. It nestled against the Pierce property where the houses were divided by a wedge of lawn and a snake rail fence. Each had a hayfield separating the residential part of the property from the road. The two families had been friends and allies in the ranching business for years—since well before she'd been born. She remembered many a sunny afternoon as soon as she'd been big enough to do so, scampering over the fence to visit with the Baylor boys, her go-to playmates as an only child.

The friendships had bloomed naturally, and it was as if she'd grown up with four brothers, always closest to Noah in both age and friendship. How things had changed.

She put on her blinker just past their red mailbox and turned into the Pierce driveway. It had been two years since she'd been home and a sense of relief washed over her for just a second before it was pushed aside by a frown. Just at the edge of the heifer barn, she could see her father's pride and joy, the John Deere tractor he'd bought just before she left, coming around the corner. He was a champion when it came to pain but there was absolutely no way he should be working the fields three days after an injury like the one her mother had reported on the phone. She'd been right to come home, even when he protested that he was just fine.

Her concern grew into something entirely different when she put her car into park and the tractor chugged into the yard in front of her. Noah Baylor turned off the tractor, lowering the hydraulic bucket and climbed down like he had been driving it for weeks. It occurred to her, he probably *had* been driving it for weeks. Or at least a few days. She'd come as quickly as she could, but her father had missed the step on this very same tractor three days ago. The ranch didn't stop just because of a silly rotator cuff.

The last image she'd had in her mind of a defeated, damaged Noah was nothing like the man who stood before her now. Damn, he looked good. Better than he had in a long time. She drew a breath that erupted in butterflies in her belly and she cursed to herself. *This is bad. Really bad.*

This was the reason she hadn't been home in two years, *this* very feeling, the pounding in her ears, the heart beating out of her chest. She'd applied to groom for Renegade Racing as a last ditch effort to stop herself from falling into the abyss of loving the Noah she'd unsuccessfully tried to keep afloat for a year, and the time away had *helped*. This, right now, proved that nothing had *changed*. She let out a shaky breath.

She couldn't stop herself from letting her eyes rake over his body, a body she'd been able to forget about over the last two years. When her last memory was him soaked in whiskey with blood on his t-shirt, it was easy to forget the tall, broad shouldered slice of cowboy that he'd grown into. His skin was bronzed as a testament to hours spent working in the sun, and he'd put on some muscle since she'd last seen him – the kind of long, lean muscle developed from use, not from lifting weights. She could see his mop of dark curls were cropped closer and plastered to his head, a nod to the hours he'd already put in today, as he took off his ball cap and held it between his hands. His standard uniform of old Justin cowboy boots, a pair of faded jeans and a fitted t-shirt was more appealing than any of the expensive Wrangler shirts and boots she saw in Denver on a day to day basis.

The buzz of attraction deep in her belly made her wonder if that last, painful year after Gavin's accident hadn't happened at all. Lord knew seeing him again after so long stirred up feelings that had been dormant for a long time.

The silly shit-eating grin he always wore was familiar, but the concern in his slate eyes sure wasn't. Cautiously, she opened the door of her car and stepped out.

"Well I'll be damned. Emma Pierce."

She couldn't help the little smile that tugged at the corner of her lips. Her head clearly hadn't caught up with her heart at the shock of seeing him on her family spread instead of his own. And that was why, when he cleared the space between them in a few sure strides, and wrapped her up in his arms, she melted into him like she had just about every day of her life. Forgetting the past for just a moment, she gave her body to his embrace, releasing the tension of two hours of driving, unsure how she'd be received after two years of absence. *Somebody* was happy to see her.

She could feel the thud of his heart against her cheek and inhaling, she drew in the comfortably familiar smell of hay and leather underscored by the masculine smell she had discovered was unique to Noah. It set off all kinds of thoughts and feelings in her brain, most of them irritatingly aroused. She took an abrupt step back when she realized her body had forgotten about the fact Noah had never come to Denver or even made an attempt to apologize for what he'd put her through. She'd thought about that a lot, as the days and then months had stretched on with no word from him. Eventually, she'd decided that she was at fault for letting him string her along for so long, and she'd forgiven herself because it was easier to do than deal with the sting of knowing he hadn't reached out to her.

"You don't look like daddy."

"Your mama called me the morning after. Said he was hollering for her to help him put his boots on so he could go feed. As it was, he followed me around for the first two days to remind me how a ranch works." He shrugged, wiped his hands on his jeans. "Actually not all that different from ours, it turns out."

"Thank you for doing this...I got away as quickly as I could. I had to wait for my manager to figure out how to shift the workload."

He shrugged her thanks off, and shook his head. "It's nothing. I've been helping Dane out over home for the last couple of months so it just rounds out my days. Didn't expect you to show up."

His comment pinched her heart and she winced. Nothing had made her more homesick than hearing her mama and daddy talk about Three

Rivers when they came to Denver and stopped by to visit her. It had been safer to stay than to confront the conflict with Noah she'd run away from.

"Just had to make sure things didn't fall apart." She managed to edge her voice with playfulness, though it was tough to resist the urge to defend herself. She was very busy and important at Renegade Racing. After all, those horses wouldn't have fed and exercised *themselves*. At least that's what she'd told herself when she missed the first Christmas. And it was the same line she fed her father when they talked on the phone and he asked if she'd be coming home for a visit anytime soon. She'd taken a page right from the book of Noah Baylor right there; letting others around her hurt while she dealt with her own pain.

"Good thing. I'm barely holding it together on my own." He was the playful Noah she knew so well but hadn't seen in years.

She had been preparing herself since she'd gotten the call from her mother. She knew she'd see him but she wasn't sure what to expect; Stephanie told her that he was *better* but Stephanie hadn't been the one answering the 3am phone calls from the sheriff, either. All she knew was she'd missed this version of him so much, it was easy to forget about the hell they'd gone through.

Noah started to speak but the sound of the door to the house opening caught them both.

All the feelings of anxiety she'd had surrounding coming home drained out of her when she saw her father's tall figure. Apart from one arm in a sling, he looked exactly as she'd left him, except instead of distraught over her departure, he was jubilant. He lifted his good arm in greeting and a broad smile covered his bearded face. She felt the smile right in the middle of her heart, loosening the pinch of Noah's words.

"Daddy!" She didn't give Noah a second thought as she raced toward Jonas Pierce. He crushed her in his best one-armed rendition of his signature bear hug and she wished she hadn't stayed away so long. They'd been to Denver just a couple of months ago, but it wasn't the same thing as seeing him here. His familiar scent of tobacco and silage filled her nose and she closed her eyes and buried her face in his shoulder. She'd come by her own nearly six foot height honestly, but he still towered over her.

"I missed you, sweetheart."

Hot tears threatened to escape and she squeezed her eyes shut to avoid them spilling. Living next door to the tragedies the Baylors had experienced should have been enough to make her come home at Christmas, but she'd been stubborn and afraid, and now she wished she hadn't been.

"I missed you too, Daddy."

Noah stood by, fiddling with his hat in his hands. "I finished getting that pen ready for the heifers. We can probably bring them down tomorrow morning," he interjected.

"Thanks, Noah." Jonas spoke over Emma's head, and she finally released herself from his embrace and turned back to Noah. It irritated her, the way her heart fluttered when she saw him. *Turns out absence—and sobering up—makes the heart grow fonder.*

He stood there for a moment longer, as if he couldn't decide to stay or go.

"It's good to see you, Em."

The intimate nickname was another shot to the heart. He was the only one she'd ever allowed to call her anything but Emma. It was like a gentle fingertip up her spine, and she couldn't decide if she welcomed it or not.

"You too, Noah."

He nodded and turned, heading over the lawn to the snake rail fence that divided the two properties, which he stepped over and made his way up to the big Baylor house. Emma and her father watched him until he was out of sight.

"You didn't tell me Noah was helping you."

Her father lifted his good shoulder in a shrug as they watched him go.

"Closest able-bodied man. He was glad to help. And the last time I checked, *I* sign the payroll checks," he teased, bumping her arm lightly.

The door behind them opened and Myrna Pierce poked her head out. "You gonna stand out there forever or are you gonna come in and give your mama a hug?" Her chiding tone only thinly veiled the emotion in her voice.

Emma lifted her head, laughed, and plowed right into her mother's embrace. They spoke on the phone once a week and had enjoyed a couple dozen visits in Denver but it wasn't the same thing, not by a long shot.

"The prodigal daughter returns." Emma could hear the smile in her mother's voice as she folded her up in her arms. Myrna's hand smoothed over Emma's ponytail and then she held her daughter at arm's length and eyed her appraisingly. "I don't know why or how, but I'll take it."

The realization that *nobody*, not just Noah, expected her to come home because of her father's injury hit her like a punch in the gut. She deserved it. Christmases, birthdays, holidays; they'd all passed and she hadn't shown her face. What would have made Jonas's tumble off the tractor and subsequent injury any different?

Emma forced a smile, but she could feel tears at the back of her throat. She hadn't expected to feel anything but relief to leave Three Rivers and the tangled mess that had become her friendship with Noah. Homesickness crept in after the newness of Denver had worn off, and she'd thought coming home would mean she'd be pulled right back into all of the pain.

As always, there was a pot of coffee perking on the counter and her mother was set up at the table with a jigsaw puzzle in the frame that Jonas had made for her so she wouldn't have to put it all away until she was completely done.

The familiar parts of the house made her breathe a sigh of relief. For two years now, she'd felt like she was walking around with her shoulders drawn up protectively but just being here drew the defensiveness out of her and she relaxed. She slid into a chair at the table, immediately finding an edge piece on her mother's puzzle board that fit into the spot where she'd left off.

"You always do that." Myrna smiled. Her mother's smile was like the old, comfortable sweater that Emma had had her whole life—she kind of forgot how cozy it was until she slid back into it and then she never wanted to take it off.

She took in her mother; two years had hardly done a thing to her appearance. Myrna was soft as a cloud and tough as nails all at once. The sort of mother that nurtured every kid who passed through her door frame with tender love but turned mama-bear the second one of them was threatened. It was what had made her long role with social services so successful. People trusted her, they loved her, and she loved them back; and when it came down to the wire, Myrna didn't take a single ounce of shit. Emma wished she had inherited that from her.

Her blonde hair was starting to show silver and she made no attempt to hide it. It made Emma proud, the way her mother embraced everything her body did naturally. She'd never been a small woman; if Emma came by her height honestly from her father, the lush curves and thick thighs had come from her mother honestly, but not once had she ever heard Myrna call herself fat, or talk about being unhappy with her body. Jonas made no secret that he appreciated his wife's curves and while Emma had found it gross when she was younger, she'd learned to ignore it when she caught him patting her mother's bottom or holding her a beat too long when he took her in his arms.

Smiling absently, she watched her mother press another piece into place. Her father slid a cup of coffee in front of her and settled in beside her. She felt the first peace she had in a long time. Home was good, even if Noah was here. Even if her heart was conflicted on that point.

TWO

DESPITE HIS GROWLING stomach, Noah dragged his feet crossing the lawn toward the Baylor house. Standing there felt wrong. Walking away felt wrong. Holding Emma in his arms for that short moment was the rightest thing he'd felt in two years. He didn't know what cosmic forces he had appeased for her to come home, but he uttered a prayer of thanks to whoever was listening.

His heart was simultaneously racing and felt like it was squeezed in a vise. He knew this feeling well. It hadn't gone away for weeks after she left and had fueled him, on the rare occasions he was sober enough, to get into his truck and start for Denver, vowing he'd make things right. Every time, he'd turn around at the highway sign and go straight back to Danny's bar and try to burn the feeling out with whiskey. He couldn't go to her in Denver because he had no business ruining something she'd wanted her entire life. But she'd come back here, that was different. What could he do to show her how sorry he was?

Rex, the resident ranch dog, met him at the fence as he stepped over it. He paused and ruffled the dog's floppy ears and the old canine leaned into his touch. The Australian Shepherd was technically his eldest brother, Dane's dog, but his loyalty lie with whoever had the most willing hand when it came down to it. His enthusiastic, bobbed-tail wiggle made Noah smile. He picked up a stick under the big oak out front and chucked it for the dog that, despite his age, bounded off happily to retrieve it.

Noah straightened, resisting the urge to look over his shoulder to catch one more glimpse of Emma, and headed for the big ranch house where his soon-to-be sister-in-law would have something on the stove. His six year old nephew, Gage, came running out of the little orchard on the other side of the driveway and Rex abandoned his stick in favor of the possibility of attention from his favorite playmate.

"Uncle Noah!" The child tore across the dooryard and directly for Noah's knees. He intercepted, catching Gage under the armpits and tossing him over his shoulder like a bag of feed. Giggling uncontrollably, Gage half-heartedly pounded his uncle's back while Rex danced around their feet. Despite losing his parents three years earlier, the child had adjusted well and retained a lightheartedness that Noah sometimes envied.

Kerri Maddock followed Gage at a much

slower pace. Despite the dramatic age difference between them, the kids had become fast friends last year when Kerri and her sister, Ren, showed up at the Baylor ranch in response to the homemaker ad Dane had put out. A few months and a close call later, the pair were an integral part of the Baylor family.

"Hey Ker. How's the store going?" She'd filled his role at the family's store in town when Dane had asked him to come back to the ranch while he and Ren prepared for their upcoming nuptials. At sixteen, Kerri was happy to be making her own money, and knowing she was under the watchful eye of his parents set Ren's mind at ease, too.

"It's fine."

Noah nodded—one thing he'd learned about Kerri was that *everything* was 'fine'...except when it came to the horses. Then everything was awesome. He didn't have the nerve to tell her that a horse could break a man's heart as quick as a woman.

"Hey, did you hear I got my learner's permit?" Kerri perked, sliding the glossy piece of driver's identification out of her jeans pocket.

"God help us all," Noah said, crossing himself exaggeratedly.

"She's gonna take me for a milkshake!" Gage shouted, his voice muffled by Noah's shirt.

"Hey, do you think you can teach me how to drive the truck and trailer?" Kerri asked as the trio mounted the porch stairs.

"Hold the phone...why don't we start with *driving* to begin with. And then we'll move on to the milkshake, and *then* the truck and trailer?" Noah bargained, holding the door open for Kerri.

The smell of one of Ren's awesome home-cooked meals met them before they rounded the corner into the kitchen. Though he appreciated the freedom and independence of the bungalow in town he'd purchased a year ago, he'd never developed much skill in the culinary arts. The seasoned pork chops searing in a cast iron pan on the stove were head and shoulders above the boxed noodle dish he'd be eating if he was at his own place right now.

He deposited a squealing Gage onto the kitchen floor. Ren turned from the stove where she'd been preparing a salad beside Dane and smiled at the little boy. She wore a tank top with a dove gray cardigan that had fallen open, exposing the barely visible bump of her midsection. If he wasn't looking for it, he would have missed it. They'd announced the pregnancy to the immediate family a month ago when they'd announced their wedding, which was coming right up. Good thing, too. At the rate she was going, they couldn't keep the secret from the generally nosy, but well-meaning population of Three Rivers for much longer.

"Go wash your hands, then come back and help Kerri, okay?"

Gage nodded and took off like a shot for the bathroom. Ren had a special rapport with the child from the first day she'd arrived at the ranch, and she'd all but legally adopted him by this point. Barring his own, Ren was the best mother figure anybody could ask for and Noah knew she'd be a natural with his new niece or nephew.

"That smells great, Ren. How's your tapeworm doing?" He teased, taking off his hat and hanging it inside the door.

Her dark eyes cut to him in the best attempt at threatening she could muster but her laugh broke its severity. She'd developed a healthy appetite and he couldn't resist teasing her about it.

"Hey, was that Emma Pierce's car I saw next door?" Dane interrupted their moment with a question Noah didn't want to answer.

He knew damn well that was Emma's car. She'd bought it with her own money and been so proud she'd driven it straight from the dealership to the Baylor ranch to show it off to her 'brothers'. Noah scowled. He just wanted a few more minutes to process the whole thing and it felt like Dane was needling him – despite the fact that neither of his brothers knew what had transpired between the two of them.

"You must be happy, hey?" Dane continued. With his back turned, he put the finishing touches on dinner and completely missed his brother's 'let's not go there' expression.

"It's nice to see her." It was all Noah trusted himself to say.

Dane twisted, raising a brow.

"Who's Emma Pierce?" Kerri asked, not looking up from where she was setting the table.

Gage had emerged from the bathroom and was 'helping', which basically equated to following Kerri with his hands full of silverware.

"She's..." Noah started.

"The best girl barrel racer we know." Dane interrupted.

That caught Kerri's attention and she looked up, her eyes bright. The horse flu was in full force. "Do you think she'd give me some lessons? I mean, you're good, Noah, but..."

"I get it, she's a girl." Noah winked at Kerri, and assembled a couple of place settings on the table opposite her. "I'll ask if she'll come watch you ride."

"Awesome."

He nodded in agreement. Awesome, indeed. More time with Emma around meant more opportunities to show her the man he'd become.

THREE

LATER THAT NIGHT, Emma slipped out of the house. Her mother and father were tucked into some reality show they had taken up watching while she had been gone. Watching them settle into the life that they had made together without her was strange, but comforting. They had new rituals and traditions, and they'd made out okay without her.

Stepping out into the dark, she tugged her unzipped hoodie around her shoulders and took in a breath. She couldn't see a blessed thing but the smell, the sound, the *feel* was enough. The open sky above was littered with thousands of stars, a sight she hadn't realized she missed until she saw it again. It made her heart ache for it, even though it was right in front of her. She felt her way down the outdoor steps, wrapped her arms around herself and headed for the barn.

Fifty seven steps to the horse barn. She'd

counted it enough times; she could have done it backwards and with her eyes closed. The sweet smell of second cut hay met her nose at the door. She ran her fingers over the old barn board and they were greeted with a rusty horse shoe she had nailed there the summer she was seventeen. It was the first rodeo season Noah had his license and their parents had, with a little bit of convincing, allowed them to drive forty five minutes to a rodeo weekend alone. It had been her first season with Alamo, and her first high point win, and he'd thrown a shoe in his last run. This shoe. They'd still won. She smiled, thinking of how that two hundred dollar check had felt like a lottery win in her pocket.

Noah had been proud. He'd swung her around like she weighed nothing, hollering like a lunatic. She'd been embarrassed at the time, but secretly relished the public show of support.

She savored the moment and the memories, closed her eyes and heard the horses inside shifting, and snuffling, the quiet chewing of evening hay. Finally, she pulled the door open and stepped inside. A huge buckskin gelding in a front stall perked his ears and nickered low to her over the half door of his stall. She knew he was just looking for an extra meal but told herself it was a happy greeting to a beloved friend. Four long strides brought her to him and she dug the carrot chunks she'd brought for him out of her pocket.

"Hey buddy."

The horse gobbled them up and then shoved his forehead against her chest. She wound her arms around his head, pressing her cheek against his forelock. She couldn't help but let out a couple of tears. It was better this way, with him here, but he'd been her steady companion for almost a decade and she'd be lying if she said she didn't miss him. A girl and her horse weren't meant to be apart like this.

"Hey."

She startled and Alamo jerked his head back in surprise. The last person she'd expected was Noah. His voice was soft as he approached.

"What are you doing here?"

"Someone's gotta feed night hay." He gestured over his shoulder.

She didn't know how she'd missed him, but she'd been lost in the warm memories of that rodeo weekend. There was a light on in the far end of the barn and a partially distributed bale of hay sat in the middle of the cement aisle.

In the dim light, she took him in, all long legs and broad shoulders. He had a ball cap on and his overgrown curls curved out underneath it, winging at his ears. Oblivious to early summer chill of the night, he wore a thin t-shirt stretched across his well-muscled chest. Even before she'd ever thought of Noah in any kind of way besides a friend, she'd known he had the kind of body girls went crazy for. And they had, all through high school. Her circle of friends had primarily consisted of Stephanie and the Baylor brothers, but lots of girls tried to get close to her in order to get close to him. He never had trouble finding a date, anyways.

There were always girls sniffing around at school, at rodeos, and at the ranch.

"Ah." She leaned over the door of Alamo's stall on her elbows, watching as he lost interest in her and turned to the hay Noah had put in there for him. Noah walked over and mirrored her stance, looking in at the horse along with her.

He was close, too close. So close she could smell leather and man and a hard day's work on him, and her heart kicked in a couple of extra beats. His arm brushed against hers and even through the heavy cotton of the hoodie, her skin raised in goose bumps.

Her body was a traitor. She was supposed to protect her heart, and here she was, practically pissing on her hocks. Noah had tried to keep her in Three Rivers when she wanted to leave. Despite their friendship and closeness, he'd betrayed her that night in her car by trying to manipulate her into giving up the one thing she needed. At least, that's what she told herself. Leaving had been a lot easier than unraveling the twisted mess they'd made.

She shifted, trying to put at least a little bit of space between them but there wasn't much room. He drew his eyes away from Alamo and she could feel them on her, burning her up. *Damnit.* Why couldn't she get a handle on herself?

Finally, she met his gaze, pressing her lips together. He was close enough they could have kissed, and for a minute, she thought about it—that he would bend his head and press his lips to hers.

She'd long ago given up on that thought, but right now she found herself wanting it as much as anything. The intensity in his eyes stole the breath right out of her, and it released in a heated hiss.

Her whole body waited, tensed, for contact she was certain would come in the next beat. Abruptly, he lifted his head, looked back at the horse and wet his lips.

"I remember when you got this guy. Like it was yesterday." He smiled when he said it and she couldn't help but think he was taking the same trip down memory lane she had when she'd come through the door with the horse shoe.

He'd stepped back far enough that she could catch a breath, but she couldn't stop thinking about how close he'd been. Heat still hung in the crisp air between them. She tried her best to shake off the haze of desire that clouded her thoughts, half mad at herself for abandoning the carefully constructed confidence she'd spent two years working on in Denver.

"You were so happy to move up from Molly."

She smiled, remembering. Molly had been her Buckshot, the old-but-reliable mount that had resided at the Baylor Ranch for as long as she could remember. Each of the Baylor boys had ridden Buckshot to start, and they'd planned to use him for their nephew, Gage.

"It was like going from a Chevette to a Ferrari." Alamo lifted his head to see what all the commotion was about when she started laughing.

"He's an older model Ferrari, now though."

~

"Aw, he's still got a lot going for him." Noah reached out and stroked a hand down Alamo's nose, speaking to the horse, hoping she didn't notice the tremble in his hands. He'd come close to kissing her. In that small space between them, the thought had been overwhelming, but he remembered all too well the way desperate impulse had worked for him the last time. "I know she's seen all those flashy, fast horses, buddy. The grass always looks greener, eh?"

Realizing that Noah had no treats, the horse turned back to Emma, content to bury his face against her chest whether she had treats or not. She rubbed the spot between his ears—Noah had seen her do it a million times, and his ears went floppy, completely relaxed, a huge sigh moving through his big body. Noah knew what that felt like. The same way it felt when they'd made contact in her yard this afternoon. Perfect. Comfortable. Emma stroked the buckskin's jowls and he rooted his head against her.

"I don't know, I think the grass right here looks just perfect."

He was sure she meant with the horse, but he let himself believe she meant he was a part of that picture, too. Watching the ease with which these two partners of a decade came back together after a prolonged absence made him hopeful that there might be something left to salvage of their own relationship.

"Me too," he said, and looked over, letting his eyes sweep over her. When had she transitioned from girl-next-door Emma to alluring, irresistible Emma? Probably when he'd been too soused to notice it. The summer before Gavin died, he'd realized she was a pretty girl, but she'd blossomed while she'd been gone. Her hair was longer, and the blonde curls were mostly contained in a messy bun. A few had escaped at her hairline and temples and framed her fair-skinned face. A gentle blush that could have been from the cool night stained her cheeks. The too-big hoodie she wore covered some of her body but the fitted dark-wash jeans showed the most delectable of her curves, her lush behind and strong, thick thighs.

There was something about how at ease and relaxed she was that was sexy as hell. She was totally in her element, just *being* with Alamo. She didn't belong in Denver, not really. She belonged right here, with him.

Lifting her eyes from Alamo, she caught his gaze. He wanted to close the distance between them and take her in his arms. It would complete this picture of how they ought to be. He had no idea where her head was, and for all he knew, she'd kick and scream if he tried to hold her. The year before she left for Denver, he'd been wasted, but present enough to know that he'd systematically destroyed their friendship and her trust. He'd take what she would allow and be grateful for this second chance he didn't deserve.

She held his eyes for a long and scrutinizing moment and then finally looked away, wetting her lips.

"Well, I guess this is goodnight. I'm exhausted." She spoke to Alamo and then planted a kiss right on the swirl in the middle of his forehead.

"Yeah, that two hour drive is tough, I hear." Noah teased her because that was what he'd always done. He straightened, uncomfortable with his uncertainty. He'd never been this far out of sync with Emma in his life. "I'll walk you to the house."

"I'm fine."

"It's dark."

She laughed. "Do you *know* how many times I've walked that path in the dark? Come on, Noah."

He didn't argue but followed her out of the barn after turning off the lights, and closed the door behind them. Walking beside her in the dark, he put his hands in his pockets to stop himself from reaching out to grab her like he might have three years ago.

When they stopped in front of the porch, she turned to him. He reached out this time, grabbing her hand and giving it a light squeeze. In the dark, he heard her let out a shaky breath.

"Well. Goodnight," she said.

He nodded, released her hand, and watched her go up the steps into the house.

FOUR

"EMMA RAE!"

Emma jolted awake at the sound of her mother's voice carrying up the stairs. It took her a moment to realize where she was. Her bleary eyes took in the shelf on the other wall filled with rodeo trophies. Tipping her head up, she caught sight of her tired face and dark-circled eyes in the dresser mirror underneath the shelf and dropped her head back on the pillow. *Ugh.*

She'd thought her first sleep in two years in the bed she'd grown up in might have been refreshing. As comforting as coming home to the embraces of her parents had been. She was wrong. Tossing and turning, she'd thought of Noah most of the night. Half mad and half aroused, she'd eventually drifted off to sleep in the wee hours, but then woke up intermittently, thinking she was going to be late for chores. Which...apparently, she was. 8:30. *Shit.*

"Emma! Daylight's wastin'!" This time, it was her father's voice from the bottom of the stairs.

"Coming, Daddy!"

Groaning, she struggled into a sitting position, pinching the bridge of her nose. Gaining her bearings, she rolled out of bed and located her duffle bag. Fresh underwear, a t-shirt and socks, and her recycled bra and jeans from the day prior would do. The scent of coffee wafting up the stairs brightened her marginally. She'd feel better with a couple of gallons of her mama's strong coffee packed away.

Taking the stairs two at a time, she stopped short in the doorway of the kitchen. In his long-established spot at the head of the table, her father sat with his normal spread—breakfast plate, coffee mug and newspaper folded into quarters. The only difference was the sling he wore on his left arm to support the damaged shoulder. Her mother was at the stove; she rarely ever sat down at breakfast, stealing bites here and there while she did prep work for the rest of the meals of the day. And sitting across from Emma's seat was Noah Baylor, his long legs stretched out under the table. He looked up from where he'd been concentrating on his mug of coffee and offered her a smile that made all of her insides jumble up in a way she didn't appreciate. For a scorching moment, she thought about the look in his eyes in the barn last night and she felt a warm flush crawl over her skin.

"Mornin'," he said.

She must have scowled back because Jonas

pulled his eyes away from the headlines long enough to look up at her standing in the doorway and gesture to her seat.

"I see your absence hasn't magically made you a morning person," her father teased.

"Not a chance."

She took her seat opposite Noah and snatched two pieces of toast from a plate in the middle of the table. Her mother immediately set a mug of coffee in front of her and Emma offered her a grateful smile. Swinging her gaze back to the man across the table, she saw him watching her with an entirely bemused expression. He could wait. She stirred a bit of cream and sugar into her coffee, took a sip and set it down.

"Good morning, Noah."

A full smile broke across his features. "I knew you'd say hello once the coffee warmed you up."

How many mornings had she woken up in a chilly tent at a rodeo with Noah unzipping her door to bring her a coffee before she'd even opened her eyes? And how many times had he said those exact words? Did he even know what he was doing, taking her back years to a time when things— feelings, specifically, were much simpler between them?

He held her in his gaze, far longer than would be acceptable in polite company, but it felt warm and comfortable and it made her feel better somehow.

She broke the eye contact first, turning to

her father. "So what's on the agenda for today?"

"Well, Noah's got everything fed up. It has been a bit since the fence has been rode and those heifers need to come down from the East pasture." Jonas grinned. "I figured you'd want to reacquaint yourself with Alamo."

Not even Noah Baylor could stop the smile when her father mentioned the horse. She could barely contain her excitement for her first ride back and if she hadn't been so drained last night, she probably would have saddled him up.

She'd had the option to bring him along to Renegade but she'd left him behind until she got to know the ropes and then realized there'd be no time or energy for personal pursuits. At least here, he'd stayed with his herd and been well taken care of.

"I'll get 'Jack and meet you outside in fifteen," Noah said with an expression on his face that looked like the cat who swallowed the canary.

FIVE

"SO TELL ME what Denver was like." Noah sat on a bale of hay with Blackjack standing nearby. The gelding was resting with his head down and one hind leg cocked in relaxation, completely oblivious to the frisson of excitement in the pit of his owner's belly.

This time yesterday, he wouldn't have bet a penny on Emma being here in front of him right now, even though Jonas had told him she'd be around. She'd stayed away this long, he hadn't figured they could count on her to turn up. But here she was. Soft and warm and everything he remembered, but better. And so far, she hadn't shredded him to ribbons the way he deserved.

He watched her move around Alamo in the cross ties in the aisle of the barn. She had always been meticulous with pre-ride grooming and today was no exception. He'd watched her bend and stretch to curry every part of the horse's already-gleaming coat, admiring the view, and now she was working over his body with a dandy brush, flicking any remaining dust away. The horse's coat looked like burnished gold. Any other day, he might have goaded her for taking her time but he was allowing his eyes to reacquaint themselves with her form and enjoying it. He'd missed her presence more than he realized.

She stopped in her work and straightened, shrugging without looking at him as she slid her hand along Alamo's spine, checking for soreness. She was attuned to every detail about her horse—it wasn't any wonder the racing outfit she worked for had kept her so close.

"Nothing to tell. Long days, hard work."

"Sounds familiar." He laughed. "Didn't have to go all the way to Denver for that."

She shrugged again, her eyes flashing to him now with a look that said the topic wasn't open for discussion. He knew better, but half the fun of their friendship was needling her.

"Oh come on, you worked with some of the top barrel racers in Colorado, there must be *something* to tell."

"It was...different. A whole different side of rodeo, I think. We just play at small beans here, but the jackpots they're riding for are huge. They even have a pool and a hyperbaric chamber for injury rehab. We thought *our* horses were expensive but some of theirs cost as much as a mortgage."

She'd chosen her words carefully, something he wasn't accustomed to. He wanted to ask her to tell him how she really felt.

"Some of those riders probably should have motocross bikes instead of horses, but who am I to judge? Nice horses, though. Poor old Alamo could never have kept up."

"Oh yeah? He's pretty fast when he's in shape." Noah tipped his head toward the horse. It was true; in the women's division, she'd always ranked at the top. Alamo was the type of horse that loved the pattern, made a tight, clean run, and was barely winded at the end. When she smiled, he knew he'd touched on a truth.

"My Ferrari, right?" She stepped into the tack room and emerged with her gear, sliding the saddle and pad onto Alamo's back.

"Exactly." With some effort, he pulled his eyes away from the image of her bending and stretching to do up the fittings on the saddle and flipped the end of his reins against the bale of hay he was sitting on to distract himself while she finished tacking up. She moved quietly around the horse, and he dropped his head into the bridle when she offered it. The pair was in perfect form, reading one another's subtle body language.

~

Riding up the property, Emma stole a look at Noah. He was a different man than the one she'd left behind, that was for sure. Maybe even different than the one she'd known before the accident. That cheeky smile he flashed at her did funny things to her insides—things she didn't necessarily appreciate. It was with an ache that she realized nothing she'd done for self-preservation in Denver had actually worked.

They rode in silence for a time, through the East pasture, along the barbed wire fence that separated the back acreage of the two ranches. It was a long ride, but relaxing, an easy incline toward the end of the property where they would check the fence.

When they came up on the two dozen heifers grazing about midway up the pasture, Noah kept riding. Emma didn't object; the quiet plodding of their horses' hooves soothed her, and the feel of Alamo's steady movement under her balanced out her soul.

After a time, Noah broke the silence. "So how long are you planning to stay?"

Emma felt the tension behind the casual question.

"They expect me back once daddy is fully functional again. I signed a three year contract." She shrugged and let out a breath, thinking of the grooms she'd left behind and a new rehabilitation patient that had come in a month ago. She knew she'd left them shorthanded and Allison, the young Canadian groom, had already texted her twice to ask questions. "I have some unfinished projects."

Noah didn't respond, and Emma filled the uncomfortable silence with words. "And that could be a few weeks, or a few months. It's hard to tell, but the doctors are hopeful."

Finally, Noah spoke. "If Jonas has his way, he'll be back on the tractor within a week. He's a beast."

Emma laughed. Her father was not only the strongest, but the most stubborn man she knew. In fact, just last night when her mother had been talking about the doctor's recommendation for physical therapy, he had rolled his eyes and dismissed it as 'hogwash'.

"Well, he's only three days in, so he's still on the good stuff for painkillers. Talk to him again in a week, he might feel differently." She lowered her rein hand and Alamo picked his way across a particularly rocky section.

They reached the East end of the properties; they stretched for miles out in either direction but this particular spot ended at the top of a valley and a lush forest stretched out below them, the Rockies framed the horizon. It was a breathtaking view and Emma had ridden to this point for peace more times than she could count. She'd forgotten what a gem she had in her own backyard. She savored it for a moment before she felt eyes on her and swung her gaze to find Noah's fixed on her.

"Never gets old, does it?"

"I didn't know how much I missed this."

"This place misses you, too."

It was Emma's turn for quiet. Pressing her lips together, she let her eyes wander back out over the beauty of the wilderness and realized she had nothing to say to him. He didn't mean the trees and the fields and the pastures had missed her. He meant the people of Three Rivers had missed her; *he* had missed her. If that was true, why had he never come to Denver? Why had he never picked up the phone or sent a text? The silence stretched longer between them now, itchy and uncomfortable. The view, while spectacular, did nothing to soothe it, and she sensed it was only going to get worse.

From the corner of her eye, she could see Noah watching her but she ignored it, trying to quiet her mind and appreciate the moment for what it was. Serene, beautiful, *home.*

After a moment, he broke the silence. "Emma?"

She glanced at him.

"Can we talk about this?" He gestured in a circle between the pair of them and all of the relaxation she'd been enjoying went skittering out of her like drops of water hitting a hot iron.

"Talk about what?" She put one calf to Alamo's flank, and, ever sensitive to her cues, the horse turned on his haunches away from Noah. She started back toward the scattered heifers at an ambling walk, but her insides were trembling. She knew he was following her before she heard him but there—there it was, the second set of shod hooves coming behind her.

"Em."

His voice was heavy with emotion and before she even realized what was happening, tears were blurring her vision and she willed them not to fall. She was grateful Alamo knew the way home because she sure as hell couldn't steer him there.

"Someday, I'm going to be able to show you how sorry I am for what I did to us."

That word. Us. What did it even mean? Decades of friendship or the stirrings of something more that had started the summer before Gavin died and stopped in its tracks with the sheriff in the front yard?

"I don't want to talk about this, Noah." She tried to straighten but her body insisted on slumping forward. Alamo slowed his steps to accommodate for her unbalanced posture.

"We've never not been able to talk about something before, Emma. Not in twenty years."

She swallowed hard, and a lump in her throat pushed back, shoving more emotion than she was willing to allow straight to the surface. Sadness, and a sharp undercurrent of...what was that? Fear? They couldn't go back to the way they had been, no matter how comfortable she could feel with him. He'd crossed a line into territory that scared the shit out of her and she didn't know how to make him uncross it. Running had made the most sense. And she'd masked it with anger, just for good measure. If they didn't talk about it, she didn't have to untangle her feelings.

"Noah, please."

Still unable to bring her eyes to his, she stared straight ahead while Alamo picked his way down through the field back toward the heifers. She regretted riding up here with him. She regretted relaxing for that quiet moment looking out over the valley and the mountains. If she worked at it, she could trace her trail of regret surrounding Noah Baylor straight back to that night in her car two years ago.

"I know talking about this will help you kill whatever guilt monster you have living inside of you but it does nothing for me. So please, for me, let's not have this conversation."

When she finally glanced over at him, he looked like she'd punched him in the gut. She pushed her lips together tightly and willed her words of regret to stay inside. It would be easy to let him get the closure he needed, be able to make the apology, to be the biddable, easy Emma he had always known. Easy, but dangerous.

"Okay," he finally said. Without a word between them, they put heels to horse and set out to gather up the heifers.

SIX

"DAMNIT, DAMNIT, DAMNIT!" Noah struggled to bring his breathing under control, driving the toe of his boot into the corner of the barn a few times. Blackjack stood by, disinterested, and Rex came running from the house to see what the trouble was.

The trouble was *Emma*. That look she had on her face when he'd tried to apologize shredded his heart. That was all him. *He* had done that to her. Shut her down like that. Maybe this was something they could have talked about if he had driven to Denver, but he had been too chickenshit to do that, and now all of the time and bad feelings that had passed between them unchecked had driven a wedge into what had been the strongest, surest friendship he'd ever had.

He planted a fist on the side of the barn. The urge to drink was overwhelming. *That's what got you into this mess in the first place, Baylor.*

He'd made more than his fair share of mistakes trying to burn his feelings out with whiskey; he'd have to figure out an alternative. He booted the barn once more for good measure and led Blackjack inside.

The second oldest Baylor brother, Finn, stood in the aisle with Ren's horse, Roxy. The mare had been suffering with an abscess for a couple of weeks and was having a hot soak to draw it out so she could begin to heal. Finn worked slowly and methodically around her; he was a hell of a horseman, and between the colts they trained every year for the Reicher outfit and the sideline Finn had working with horses that nobody else would touch, he kept the equine end of the Baylor ranch afloat nearly single-handedly. He straightened and slid a hand down Roxy's neck, speaking under his breath to her in a soothing tone. He was always talking to the horses, like they understood him.

Noah led Blackjack into his stall and removed his bridle, careful not to knock the horse's teeth with the bit when he spit it out. The gelding immediately moved to his pile of hay in the corner while Noah worked at the latigo to loosen and remove his saddle.

Finn appeared in the door of Blackjack's stall with his arms crossed, an unimpressed expression covering his features.

"What the hell are you trying to tear my barn down for?"

"It's nothing, Finn."

"It's not nothing. I heard you cursing out

there."

Noah's jaw worked as he folded the latigo back into itself on the ring of Blackjack's saddle and lifted it off of the horse's back, pushing past his brother. Finn had watched him go off the deep end after Gavin's accident without a word, but had stepped in when it became clear that Noah was cutting a path of destruction through the whole town, not just his own life. Typical of an older, wiser brother, Finn asked the tough questions and made Noah answer.

Though he wasn't interested in a deep, philosophical conversation about why he waited all those years to try to tell Emma he loved her, he knew he'd slipped publicly enough that he'd have to answer to *someone* and better it was Finn who had caught his outburst than Gage or Kerri.

He slid the saddle onto the empty rack around the corner and turned back to his brother, who had followed him. "I fucked things up with Emma."

Finn's level gaze betrayed no emotion. There wasn't much he could tell Finn these days that would produce a surprised response. When Emma left, it had been Finn who worked damage control, picking up Noah's messes when he should have been allowed to grieve for his wife.

"Good job, she's been home, what? Forty eight hours?"

If he expected sympathy or support when it came to Emma, Noah should have known better. She was practically Finn's little sister and had been for all of their lives, from the time she'd started crossing the snake rail fence to see if anyone could come out and play, to the countless gymkhana nights and rodeos Dane and Finn had hauled them to with their horses before Noah had his license. People in town even occasionally called her the 'Baylor daughter'. While her relationship with Noah had been the strongest, the most intimate, it didn't stop Dane and Finn from seeing her as a younger sibling and they weren't afraid to protect her when necessary, even if it was from him.

"No, before today, I messed it up."

Finn stopped, narrowing Noah in his gaze. He'd seen the protective side of Finn come out when it came to the women in his life—Emma, Sunny, even Kerri and Ren had gotten it from time to time in their travels—it wasn't something Noah was interested in butting against.

"What do you mean?"

"When she left for Denver. She pulled me out of the sheriff's office two nights before she left."

"So she finally got sick of bailing you out?"

Noah considered his next words carefully. "Well, that, and...I tried to get her to stay. All she wanted to do was leave. And I asked her to stay."

"You clearly didn't just 'ask her to stay', based on the way she hightailed it out of here and never looked back. You know her mama's heart was broken that first Christmas she never came home." Finn shifted, arms still crossed over his chest. He was well accustomed to Noah's drawn out confessions.

"I told her I loved her."

"You *what*?" Finn's face and tone showed his disappointment as clearly as if he'd had a neon sign installed over his head indicating it.

"I told her how I felt about her."

"Stinking drunk in the middle of the night, you dropped a bomb like that on her and expected her to do anything other than run?"

Noah wiped a hand over his face. Finn's arms had unfolded and he'd balled his fists at his sides; he knew he'd be lucky if his brother didn't take a swing at him. His older brother wasn't violent, but there had been a couple of occasions when he was sobering up that required a well-timed poke in the face to drive the point home.

"It was stupid..."

"You're damn right, it was stupid. Tryin' to draw that little girl into your shitstorm right when she was about to make a break for it. That's not even fair. You know that girl would do anything for you."

"I didn't say it was fair..."

"Honest to Jesus, Noah."

"I know."

"You're lucky she'll even look you in the eye."

"I *know*."

Finn pinned Noah in his gaze for just a little longer then cussed under his breath, shook his head, and turned back to Roxy. The horse had been waiting patiently in the crossties.

Noah stood where he was for a moment

and then filled a bucket with water for Blackjack and hung it in his stall. Suddenly, Finn appeared in the door of the stall again, jabbing his finger in his brother's face.

"Don't you hurt that girl again, Noah. I mean it. You do whatever you have to, but you make it right, and you make it stick. You hear me?"

Convinced that Finn's killer right hook was coming, Noah took a step back against his horse, his hands raised in innocence. Nine times out of ten, he ceded these days to keep the peace. He couldn't blame Finn for his lingering anger over the last few years. Finn had supported him when it should have been the other way around. Despite his tough-love method for Noah's problems, he was lucky Finn cared as much as he did.

"Jesus, Finn. Calm down. I'm trying to fix it."

Turns out that hurts as much.

SEVEN

EMMA'S PHONE BUZZED from where it was face down on her bedside table and she picked it up. A thank you from Allison for the advice she'd given on Encore's ongoing treatment, and an excited text from her best friend Stephanie, advising she was ten minutes out.

She could barely wait to see her friend. Almost as close to her as Noah, Stephanie Turner had spent a lot of time at the Pierce ranch, the two of them suffering from only child loneliness. Steph had even made the trek to Denver several times in the last two years for girls' weekends and a little bit of normalcy.

She shot back a quick text and then smiled at her reflection in the mirror and smoothed her long blond hair down over the straps of her tank top. Karaoke at Danny's was exactly what she needed to get the twisted feeling out of her gut. She and Stephanie and Noah had been frequent patrons, but tonight he wasn't invited.

He wanted to talk, but she wasn't ready. She was still trying to come to grips with the way her body responded to him in that close moment in the barn. For all appearances, he seemed to be back to the normal guy she'd known before Gavin died, not the whiskey-soaked shell of a man she'd left here. It made her ache to erase the last three years.

Finally satisfied with her appearance, she slid her phone into her pocket and took the stairs two at a time. She crossed through the kitchen and poked her head into the living room, where her father was tucked into his recliner with a newspaper in hand.

"I'm going to karaoke. Don't wait up." She crossed the carpeted floor and pressed a kiss to his cheek.

"I won't." He reached up with his good arm and gave her a squeeze as she heard a knock at the door.

"That's Steph. Love you, Daddy."

"Love you, too, sweetie."

When Emma pulled the door open, Stephanie launched into her arms.

"You have no idea how excited I am! Jamie even made supper for the kids. You're never going back to Denver. We need to do this every week!"

Laughing, Emma pulled back, rolled her eyes, and waved to her father before shutting the door behind them. Looping her arm into Stephanie's, they hurried off the porch and to her running car.

Ten minutes later, Emma found herself crushed in a warm bear hug as Cutter Anderson, the resident bartender, nearly lifted her off of her feet.

"I heard a rumor you were hanging around." He chuckled, tugged her hair lightly before he went back behind the bar as she and Stephanie each pulled up a stool. "First round's on me. What are you having, girls?"

Emma spun her stool around once to take in the atmosphere. The décor hadn't changed, not that she expected it to—it hadn't in all the years she'd known about the place. It was dark and loud and there was already a half-cut regular on the microphone. If this played out anything like the fond memories she had, they would watch, amused, until the right amount of alcohol had been consumed and then she and Stephanie would bust out one of the enthusiastic done-me-wrong-song duets they had been known for.

"Whiskey!" Stephanie nearly shouted.

Cutter laughed and shook his head as he retrieved two shot glasses and set them down on the bar in front of the girls. As an afterthought, he pulled out a third and filled them, raising his glass to theirs, and the three of them threw the alcohol back.

EIGHT

"WHAT THE...?"

Noah rolled over and checked the clock. 2am. He hadn't seen this time of day in a long time, and here his phone was ringing like a bastard. He cussed again and rolled up into a sitting position; he couldn't go back to sleep and ignore it. Wiping a hand over his face, he picked up the phone and squinted at the caller display. Emma. Suddenly he was awake, very awake, and his heart played staccato at the base of his throat. Emma wouldn't be calling him in the middle of the night unless it was an emergency. He punched at the green button to accept the call.

"Em?!"

"Hey Noah...I'm sorry to call but we *really* need you down here at Danny's."

The voice on the line was slurring and unrecognizable at first; definitely not Emma's. Loud music filled the earpiece. Panic seized his gut. He checked the caller ID again to confirm it was Emma's phone, and then it dawned on him.

"Stephanie?"

"Yeah."

"Is everything okay? Is Emma alright?"

He heard giggling on the other end of the line and breathed a sigh of relief; he was already halfway into his jeans.

"We drank too much. Cutter won't let us leave."

In the background, Emma shouted. "We have whiskey!"

Finally, things started to make sense. Sunday night. Karaoke at Danny's. One of Emma's favorites in the years they'd spent raising hell between high school and her departure for Denver. He'd always gone with the girls but they clearly hadn't invited him this time.

"Yeah. I'll be there in ten. Does Jamie know where you are?"

"Shhhh...he has to work in the morning." Stephanie cut herself off giggling.

Running a hand through his hair, Noah let out a breath.

He heard Emma say *I told you so* in the background.

"You girls just stay put, okay? I'll be right there. Give Cutter..."

"Okay, bye!"

The phone went dead in his ear. He cussed for what had to be the sixth time and thumbed through the contact list on his phone, squinting at the tiny names. Selecting one, he held the phone to his ear. Emma knew how to get him out of bed, that was for sure.

"I thought you'd call." Cutter Anderson's voice was nearly overridden by the same music he'd heard from Emma's phone.

"Yeah. Can you just make sure they don't try to leave?"

"Hi Noah!" Emma's voice was shrill on the other end of the line.

"Don't worry, they're both sitting here at my bar. Right in front of my face."

"I'm on my way."

He disconnected the call and groaned at his sore muscles, pulled his jeans the rest of the way on and found himself a hoodie and ball cap. Sure, he lugged feed and did physical work at the store but it wasn't the same as trying to keep an even keel at two ranches. He'd even been staying at Dane's, in the big house, to save commuting time and give himself a few extra minutes of sleep each day – plus, Ren brewed a mean cup of coffee. Now that Emma was home, he appreciated that little bit of closeness even more.

As he crept down the stairway, through the quiet house and out into the kitchen, he couldn't help but think that Emma must have felt this way dozens of times. Two in the morning sucked, but he'd do this a million times and come back for more to try to make up for the way he'd treated her.

Rubbing his hands together in the crisp

night air, he climbed into his truck and turned the key in the ignition. Had he been at his own place in town, it would have been a stroll down the street and he could have easily had the girls crash on his couch. Guiding his truck out their rural road and then onto the main road into town, he thought about Emma, this grown up version of her, on his couch...in his house. He couldn't get the idea of her leaving town again out of his head. It didn't make sense that he'd been given this opportunity to make things right with them and then he wouldn't be able to make it happen.

Noah sidled his truck up to the curb in front of Danny's and shifted into park. All of the late night patrons were gone and he saw only Cutter's truck and Stephanie's car in the parking lot. He frowned and turned his truck off, got out and left it unlocked behind him.

The bar was older than he was, and as the only drinking hole in Three Rivers, it was frequented by any and all who wanted a beverage—young and old alike, there were no preferences. If you weren't at the dance hall on a Friday night, you were at Danny's. The green glass windows and neon open sign were all too familiar to him, but he hadn't crossed the threshold in a year or so. Straightening his life out meant he still had the occasional beer with the boys, but that was about it.

Steeling himself with a deep breath, he pushed the door open and found Cutter drying glasses behind the bar and Emma and Stephanie wilted over glasses of what looked like ginger ale.

Emma perked when she saw him, sitting up and waving.

"Noah!"

He couldn't help but smile at the sight of her, with her hair hanging down her back, wearing a low cut cotton tank top and jeans. Apart from prom, the only times he'd seen her in anything but jeans were funerals and weddings. She could have been the same Emma from three years ago, looking like this, but he knew she wasn't. She was wiser, warier, more careful—at least with him; she'd proven that when she'd shut him down in the pasture. She slid off of her stool and teetered toward him, walking slowly then quickly, and then falling over her own feet and into his arms. He caught her and she wrapped her arms around his neck, laughing.

"I knew you'd come."

"I did, too," he said, laughing.

Stephanie waved from her bar stool, where she was busy sucking back her drink through a straw.

Cutter shook his head, an amused smirk on his features. The man was good-natured; he had to be in his line of work. For as many times as he'd had to deal with drunk, belligerent, sad Noah, he still greeted his old friend with a smile.

"Are you girls giving Cutter a hard time?" He guided Emma back to her stool, but stood behind her. She leaned back against the front of him and he caught a whiff of her lemongrass shampoo. He put his hands on her shoulders to steady her and she pressed her head back on his chest.

"No! He gave us more whiskey." Stephanie waved at her glass and Noah raised a brow at Cutter.

"Ginger and whiskey. Heavy on the ginger." He held up his fingers to indicate that he may or may not have put the tiniest smidge of liquor in the drinks. If Noah knew him half as well as he thought he did, Cutter had cut the girls off an hour ago. He'd played that one over on Noah more than once.

"I appreciate it, Cutter." Noah met his old friend's eyes. As with just about everyone else in town, there had been times in the last couple of years when they didn't see eye to eye but an apology over a beer had brought Cutter around.

"Hey, no problem, buddy." Cutter turned to the window, flicked off the open sign and turned to his till. Noah had closed out Danny's as many times as Cutter had, probably, his nose in a beer, waiting for Emma to come get him. Those were the good nights, if they could be classified as such, compared to the worse ones, like right before she'd left.

"Alright, girls." Noah squeezed Emma's shoulders lightly.

Stephanie pouted. "Come on, do we haveta?"

Noah helped Emma off of her stool, unsurprised at Stephanie's reaction. She was as straight-laced as they came most of the time, but once you got her started, she always had a good time and hated to see it end.

"Yes, you 'haveta'. Jamie will be calling the cops when he rolls over and you aren't there. Plus, I'm sure Cutter would like to get home sometime before dawn."

Cutter nodded exaggeratedly in response.

"You're a party pooper." That was Emma. She'd gotten to her feet but she had an arm tightly around his waist and her big blue eyes were drooping. Historically, she had a few good hours once she got into the booze, and then she crashed, hard. Often, she'd go to her tent without telling anyone or he'd find her curled up in a corner or on a bale of hay with no muss or fuss. Honestly, he was impressed she had lasted this long. "We were just getting started."

"I'm sure you were." He laughed, slid Stephanie under his other arm and the trio made for the door. "Thanks again, Cutter."

"See you around, Noah." Cutter shook his head and laughed, turning back to counting his till.

It wasn't easy but Noah guided them out the door and onto the sidewalk. The few feet to the truck weren't a problem but getting either girl into the pickup was going to be a challenge.

"I think I'm gonna be sick," Stephanie muttered.

"Alright, that means Emma's in the middle." He deposited Stephanie to support herself against the bed of the truck and opened the door, edging Emma toward it.

"Alright, alright." She grumbled, swatted at his hands, and attempted to crawl into the truck.

Noah cursed himself again for not having running boards. He watched her struggle for a minute before he put his hands on her waist and gave her a push, depositing her, with a shriek of laughter, onto the seat.

"Now get over, Steph's gotta get in," he directed.

Emma made a big show of wiggling into the middle and Stephanie moved to stand in front of the door. She gave Noah a pointed look, her eyebrows raised.

"There will be no manhandling me. Jamie would *not* be happy."

Noah laughed out loud. Like just everybody their age in this tiny town, he'd gone to school with Jamie Turner and he wasn't afraid of him. He suspected Jamie would be thrilled that he got Stephanie home in one piece, no matter what methods were employed to do so.

"Okay then, get in on your own." He nodded to the truck, and the petite brunette gave him a haughty sigh. What she lacked in stature she made up for with sass.

It took a few minutes of struggling but eventually, with Emma pulling on her hand, Stephanie managed to get herself into the truck, giving him a spiteful look as she settled herself in.

"*You* need running boards."

"I'll have them installed tomorrow just for chauffeuring drunk girls. Seat belts." He laughed, closing the door gently on her, and crossed around the front of the truck to slide in behind the wheel.

The truck wasn't designed for three adults to begin with and Emma had gotten over too far. He wasn't even going to bother trying to move her back over toward Stephanie, who had rolled down the window and was hanging her head out. Their bodies pressed tight and Emma, warm and soft, curled into his side like it was the most natural thing to do. He slipped his arm over her shoulder to make space for her and drew her closer. Under different circumstances, that would have been exactly where he'd want her. Hell, no, even under these circumstances, this was exactly where he wanted her. Drunk, but safe.

Turning the key in the ignition, he shook his head. He deserved this. At least the girls were in good humor. He couldn't say the same for himself every time Emma had picked him up. If he didn't sneak away to sleep it off on the bench seat of his truck, he was loud and rowdy and Cutter called her, or when he was beyond what Cutter could do for him, Banks picked him up and held him until she came. He wasn't proud of that period in his life, and he figured even if he had to pick up Emma drunk and silly every night for the rest of her life, it probably wouldn't pay back what he'd put her through.

They pulled away from the curb and Noah drove slowly down the main drag of Three Rivers. It was all but a ghost town after nine o'clock, abandoned save for Danny's patrons until the bar closed.

Across from Sawyer's Grocery, he turned

off at Turner's Gas station and down a private road, dotted by a few houses. Stephanie and Jamie had grown up across the street from each other—their parents operating two of the key services in town—and had been playmates through school. They had two little boys not yet in school and a sweet little life he hadn't imagined himself wanting until he pulled up to the little house with the porch light still on. He saw the curtain beside the living room window drop back and looked over at Stephanie, who was green around the gills.

"I'd say Jamie waited up." He nodded toward the house as her husband stepped out onto the porch in pajama pants and bare feet. She scoffed as she watched him approach and opened the door, nearly tumbling into his arms. He folded her up in his arms.

"Hey Noah."

"Jamie." Noah nodded.

"Thanks for bringing her home."

Noah tipped the brim of his ball cap. "I couldn't have left them there...though that one might have let me if she couldn't get into the truck unassisted."

Jamie tucked Stephanie under his arm, pressing an affectionate kiss to the top of her head. They were crazy in love and had been for years now. Through family deaths, births, and other challenges, there seemed to be nothing that could pull the pair apart and Noah admired it. Wished for it for himself, these days.

"I hope she didn't give you too much

trouble..."

Just then, Stephanie retched and vomited on the ground at her husband's feet. Amusement crinkled the corners of Jamie's eyes as he smoothed her long hair back away from her face.

"Good luck with that." Noah laughed.

Jamie stepped back and closed the door, waving as Noah shifted into reverse.

He backed out of the Turners' driveway, sliding his arm along the back of the seat to look over his shoulder. Emma curled in tighter, crossing an arm around his waist and tucking it into the seat belt near the door. He could have done without the distraction but damnit if it didn't feel right for her to be there, pressed up against him. He dropped his hand off the back of the seat and rested it on her hip, drawing her closer as he pulled away from the Turner house.

"Em?"

"Mmm?"

"Where am I taking you?"

"Mmm."

He considered his options. Wake her family, or his, or—safer yet—take her back to his place in town and return her in the morning when he went to the ranch. He made the executive decision, turning right at the end of the main drag and heading back to his bungalow.

His headlights swept over the front of the house. He'd been seeing very little of it the last few weeks. Shifting into park, he eased himself out of Emma's grip. She slid down his body until her head was resting on his thigh and he was half out of the truck. Carefully, he lifted her head and set it down on the seat. She was just about out; he'd be lucky to get her in the house and into bed before she was down for the count.

She was still present enough to lift her head when he opened the passenger door and tapped her hip lightly.

"Come on, sweetheart."

Grudgingly, she dragged herself into a sitting position, clearly sleepy and confused. "Are we home?"

"Nah, I brought you to my place. I'll take you home in the morning when I go to feed."

"Okay." She slid out of the seat slowly and he steadied her until her feet hit the ground, then tucked her against his chest and shut the door behind them.

"This doesn't look like the big house," she mumbled.

She'd never been here; this had been a part of making things right with his brothers. At that point, they were so sick of cleaning up his messes, he had decided if there were any more left to make, they ought to be made out of their sight. Plus, it was just a jaunt around the corner to the store where he'd been working for his parents.

"No, this is the place I bought after you left."

She lifted her head and looked up at him. "You bought a house?"

He nodded, unlocked the front door and

guided them through it. "I did. After you left."

"You're not the same Noah."

They entered the living room and he flicked on the lamp on the end table.

"I'm the same, just smarter."

"Hmm."

He ignored her pensive remark and moved from her side to turn on the light in the bathroom, gesturing.

"Bathroom's here, bedroom..." He stepped into the door of the bedroom to turn on the light in there as well. "...right here. You'll want to get some shut eye. 5am is gonna come early."

The lights seemed to have brought her about a little bit and she shut herself in the bathroom while he busied himself getting blankets and a pillow for the couch and made himself a bed there. Straightening as he heard the toilet flush, he looked around the small home he'd made his own. For a time, it had felt like a haven—a place to work through his demons away from the prying eyes of his family. To do what he wanted without Finn's disapproval. To mourn for Gavin and Sunny and then Emma. Now, having spent time back on the ranch with his family and Emma's, it felt stark and lonely.

When she emerged from the bathroom, he looked up and drew a tight breath. She'd taken off her jeans and was standing in the doorway in just her tank top and panties. Over a lifetime of friendship, he'd seen her in various states of undress but the scant clothing led him all too quickly to think of the little bit it was hiding. It wasn't right, not right now, but he was a hot blooded man and the memory of her warm body curved around his in his truck was still too fresh. He cleared his throat and nodded toward the bedroom door.

"Go on, it's all yours. Take a little nap and then we'll put you in bed at home."

She looked at the couch, frowning. "Where are you sleeping?"

"I'll just be right out here." He gestured to the couch.

"That's not fair. I'll sleep out here."

"No, Em, it's fine. Just go get some rest." With the couch between them, he had some safe space. She took a couple of steps toward him and he instinctively backed up.

"I'm not putting you out of your own bed."

"It's no problem, Em, honestly."

She cocked a hip and he groaned. This girl would be the absolute death of him, and he would deserve every bit of it.

"Come share. It's not like we haven't shared a bed before."

He let out a tight breath. Things were different then. He wanted to hold out on this but the longer they spent arguing about it, the less sleep he was going to end up getting and tomorrow would be a long day. Either way, he knew he was kidding himself if he thought he'd get any rest with her in the same bed.

"Okay, fine. No funny business though."

She laughed and raised three fingers beside her head. "Scout's honor."

Cute. He rolled his eyes and edged toward the bedroom. She slipped inside and he followed, willing his eyes not to travel to her cute, round ass. Was she switching her hips like that on purpose? *Get your shit together, Baylor.* He rubbed a hand over his face and closed the door behind them.

She pulled back the covers and climbed in while he pulled off his jeans and hoodie and followed suit as quickly as he could. He stretched out on his back and folded his hands under his head, averting his eyes as she did her typical nighttime nesting routine, fluffing the pillow, turning onto her side, then her stomach, and pulling the blankets up to her chin, then tucking them under her arms. She huffed and he smiled to himself—typical Emma. She was like old Rex trying to get to sleep. Had to circle a few times before she could settle in.

He reached out to the bedside table and flicked the lamp off. One of Three River's mere two dozen streetlights cast a shadow through his blinds, across the bed. The queen mattress left lots of room for them to sleep without touching but he could feel the weight of her body on the other side. He couldn't have been more aware of the fact she was in his bed if she had been curled up next to him, skin to skin. And then suddenly, she was. He felt her shiver and then her chilled fingers at his waist before she closed the space between them, sliding up against his side, resting her head on his shoulder. They'd probably mirrored this pose a dozen times in their lifetime, but never with this little clothing between them, and never with her fingers sliding over his abdomen like *that*. He bit back a groan as they came to rest just inches above the waistband of his boxers. Her cool skin against his did nothing to combat the way his blood heated thinking of her slipping her fingers just a little lower...

"Em."

He turned his eyes to the ceiling and swallowed hard, tightening his jaw. She wiggled closer, her head moving to his chest, her ear right above his thundering heart, her thighs pressed against his hip. He didn't dare look at her.

"Yeah?"

"Em, you're killing me."

Instead of responding, she slid her leg over the top of his, twining them together. A couple inches further and she'd realize how much these little things turned him on. The softness of her body pressed against his was so damn hot. And she was drunk. Out of her mind.

He wanted to kiss her. Since she'd come home the idea had settled in the back of his mind and it wasn't going anywhere. Now, it was joined by the idea of doing a multitude of other things to her. But not like this. Not when she wouldn't remember it. Not when he'd be taking advantage of her drunkenness.

When her fingers slipped lower still and brushed the little bit of clothing he wore, he rolled abruptly onto his side and tugged her tight to his body, clenching his jaw. He had to control the situation somehow, or they'd both be dealing with the type of morning-after regret he was all too familiar with. He trapped her arms against her sides to contain those roving hands—if they went where she thought they were going, he'd be a goner.

"This is just the whiskey talking, sweetheart."

"No." Her voice was muffled against his chest, but he could still hear every ounce of defiance in it. She tipped her head up and he felt her hot little mouth move across his jaw and then land on his throat. He closed his eyes and slid a hand into her hair, twisting his fingers into the long, silky waves. The temptation to give in to her was overwhelming, but he finally regained self-control and pressed a kiss to the top of her head.

"I know what you think you want and there is no way in hell I'm going to let it happen. You'll hate me in the morning. And yourself."

She stilled with her face pressed in the crook of his neck.

"Besides, you promised no funny business. Scout's honor."

She didn't respond, and within a few seconds he could hear her even breathing and feel the still, heavy sleep in her body. Just like Em. In so many ways, she was everything he remembered her to be, but in so many ways she wasn't. Relieved he was able to wait her out, he loosened his grip into a gentle embrace, buried his face into his pillow and hoped for sleep.

NINE

EMMA SCOOPED A handful of cold water from the bathroom faucet and splashed it on her face, then leveled with herself in the mirror and winced. She looked like hell and felt even worse; a feeling that was only exacerbated by the soft tap that came at the door next.

"Em? We gotta roll. Critters are hungry." His voice was gentle and he hadn't said a thing about her behavior mere hours before, but she still felt a flush creep up her neck just knowing he was out there.

She'd managed to crawl out of the bed and flee to the bathroom before he'd even turned off his alarm. It was useless to pretend she didn't remember anything because of her state of sobriety, because he'd remember everything. Pressing her damp fingers against her closed eyes, she wished he'd just go away, but knew there was no way that would happen. She was at his house, for crying out loud. *His* house, off the ranch. It was something she'd never thought she would see; the idea of carefree, smart-ass Noah remembering to pay property taxes and buy house insurance was almost laughable.

"Yeah." Opening her eyes, she drew in a long breath, held it in her cheeks and then let it out in a slow, loud puff. She remembered, too. Everything. Worse, she was a little turned on by the memory. He hadn't pushed her away; he'd actually drawn her *closer*. And he'd been turned on too, she'd felt it when he'd pressed her against the hardness of his body. Her mind wandered, against her will, to the barely defined ridges over his abs, and the little trail of hair her fingers had followed to the band of his shorts. She felt a pang low in her belly and blushed again.

Steeling herself, she turned and pulled open the door. Noah had slid on a pair of boots and a ball cap and looked considerably more rested than she felt. He handed her a hoodie and she tugged it on over the jeans and tank that she'd recycled from the night before. Next, he handed her a couple of white painkillers and a glass of water, and when she dispensed with that, a full travel mug. She smelled the top of it, raising a brow at him.

"Peppermint tea. Mama stocked me up, said it helps with queasy stomachs. I never tried the stuff."

"Thanks."

"It's alright, girl. We'll get you home and in bed and you can snooze a few more hours."

"I should be helping you feed." She groaned. The mere idea of the sickeningly sweet smell of silage, which she normally loved, did not agree with her queasy stomach.

He pulled the door open and gestured for her to go ahead. "I'm sure I can handle it this morning," he said.

She stuck her tongue out at him as she passed through the door, but the closeness made the heat in her cheeks flare up again.

"I did it for three days before you got here." He grinned, following her out and locking the door behind him. "I could do it on my own, but I like the company."

"Jerk," she muttered.

Their easy banter felt like cool water on a fresh burn, relief for the itchy aching. He could have teased her mercilessly about her attempt to literally get into his pants, but he didn't. Maybe they *could* go back to where they'd left off before Gavin's accident.

Stepping out into the cool, dark morning, she was grateful for the warmth of his hoodie. She wobbled toward his truck, still unsteady and maybe a little more inebriated than she initially thought. Without warning, she felt his hand at the small of her back, steadying her and guiding her toward the truck. His big body was warm and close and she briefly considered abandoning her shame and hauling him back into that huge bed in the house to nestle into the heat of his body and the comfort of their friendship.

He opened the door of the truck for her and offered her a crooked smile. "You gonna need a lift again?"

For what felt like the hundredth time, she flushed, remembering his hands on her waist, then the way she'd pressed herself into him, maybe a little on purpose.

"No," she said ruefully and reached for the handle on the door frame to lift herself into the truck. Her whole body screamed out, including her stomach, which flip-flopped at the quick movement. Her face contorted. There was little she hated worse in the world than throwing up, and she was known to do just about anything to avoid it.

Noah dropped his hand on her knee lightly. "You gonna be okay?"

"Yeah." She responded through clenched teeth.

"No chucking in the truck, alright?"

Despite the questionable state of her stomach, she smiled. The truck was his baby, and he'd saved up rodeo earnings from the time he was sixteen to buy it. It was at least six or seven years old by now but he'd taken good care of it. It looked like it had hardly worked a day in its life, unlike the ranch trucks they seemed to go through every few years.

She took a sip of the tea he'd made for her. She wasn't sure it actually helped, but the warmth in her stomach made her feel a little more human.

"Alright."

~

The ride through the sleepy streets of Three Rivers was so quiet Noah had to check a couple of times to make sure Emma was still upright. She was clutching that travel mug like her life depended on it, taking the tiniest sips. She was either being polite or the tea, which he personally thought smelled like someone's used up chewing gum, was doing the trick.

"How you making out?"

He heard her let out a long breath.

"I'm sorry, Noah."

What the hell? He glanced at her again, raising a brow. Of all the out of character things Emma had done in the last eight hours, this one probably took the cake.

"What the hell are you sorry for?"

"This. I woke you up in the middle of the night, disrupted your life..."

"Em. You don't owe me anything, least of all an apology." Even if she *had* crafted this as some strange sort of revenge, he would have deserved it.

"I just wanted to have a good time with Steph. Oh God, I'll have to call and check on her. She was in a bad way when we left her, wasn't she?"

Thinking of the scene when they'd dropped Stephanie off last night, he shook his head, grinning a bit.

"I thought you were joking about the whiskey."

She snorted through her nose, then

blanched and sat back like she was trying to avoid repeating her friend's retching outside his truck.

"I never joke about whiskey." She deadpanned, and he laughed.

"Yeah, you're right on that one."

They passed the Baylor ranch driveway and he turned into the Pierce's. A short way up the drive, they could see lights were on. She'd dragged her feet long enough that her parents would be up and curious.

Noah put the truck in park in front of the house and turned off the engine but Emma didn't move.

"This doesn't look good."

Noah laughed and climbed out of the truck. "For once, it's not my fault."

She let out a noise of protest, opening her door. He was waiting to help her out, but she sat for a second longer. Finally, she shifted, gingerly sliding herself off the seat and onto the ground. He steadied her.

"*I'm* not going in the house." He shook his head, guiding her toward the porch steps. "That one's all on you."

She cursed. "Why is he even awake? He doesn't have to feed."

Noah shrugged, but he was barely containing his amusement at the entire situation. "Go on in, then."

He stood and watched her go, shaking his head with a smile still on his face. If nothing else ever amounted from the way she'd folded her body around his the night before, it had at least broken the stiffness between them. He could live with that.

TEN

EMMA WOKE NEAR noon with a headache so bad she could hear her brain knocking with her pulse. She groaned and pressed her finger to her eyelids, then realized the knocking was coming from her bedroom door.

"Come in." With a throat as dry as kindling, her voice barely worked. She resisted the urge to pull the covers over her head when Noah poked his head in. All of the alcohol was gone from her body now, and his face brought the full realization of what she'd done back to her quickly.

"I thought you were my mom."

"She took your dad to his doctor's appointment."

"Shit, I promised him I'd take him!" She tried to sit up but was stopped by what felt like a machete blade right between her eyebrows. As she settled back against the pillows, Noah crossed the floor and put a cup of coffee on her bedside table.

"I told her you'd overdosed on fun." He smiled and held out his closed hand. When she put hers under it, he dropped a couple more painkillers into her palm. "She understood."

"Did she tell you to check and make sure I'm still alive?" Carefully, Emma slid herself a little more upright in the bed, making space for Noah by her legs.

"No, that was for my own peace of mind." He settled on the edge of the bed.

Emma picked up the coffee mug, stuck the pills under her tongue and swallowed them with a mouthful. Though he knew exactly how she took it, he'd mixed her coffee a bit creamier and sweeter than normal and she let out a contented breath through her nose, closing her eyes.

"This is the best coffee of my life." She croaked. "You're my hero."

When he laughed, his eyes crinkled at the corners. That was new. Three years seemed to have aged him more than it should have, but it was alright. He looked less like the sad mess of a boy she'd left behind and more like a man who could handle what life served him.

"You're full of shit, but I'll accept that compliment."

She laughed out loud, wrapping both hands around the mug and letting its warmth seep into her fingers. She met his eyes through the steam coming from the coffee.

"Really, Noah. Thank you for looking after me last night."

He shook his head, brushing off her seriousness. "It was nothing, really. But if you insist on paying me back, I know what you can do."

"Go on," she said, preparing herself for a repeat of the non-conversation in the pasture. She would have deserved it. She would avoid it for as long as she could, but she knew he wouldn't let this go on forever. He'd find a way to say the things he wanted to say; he always did.

"You can be my date to Dane's wedding."

"It's this weekend right?" The thought of him all dressed up in a suit made her stomach twist in a way that definitely wasn't the hangover.

He nodded. "Saturday."

She let out an exaggeratedly long-suffering sigh and then finally nodded. "I guess I owe it to you."

His smile widened. "You won't be sorry."

"As long as I don't drink as much as I drank last night." She laughed. With the coffee in her system and the painkillers starting to kick in, she was beginning to feel a little less like death. She stretched her legs under the blankets and wiggled her toes.

"Don't worry, Cutter is tending the bar. If he knows what's good for him, he'll remember how much is 'too much'."

"Between the two of you, I suspect my whiskey intake will be highly monitored." She smiled, taking another swig of the coffee. Her stomach was starting to rumble and that was a good thing.

"Damn right. Now, you think you're up for putting something in that belly?"

"Are you offering to cook me something?" She tipped her head and observed him through narrowed eyes. He'd changed a lot but she would be shocked if his cooking skills had improved also.

"No. I'm going to take you to Hinkley's. Because even though my skill in the kitchen has improved, I just don't think you're ready for that yet." He teased, and then rose to his feet.

"What about chores?"

"Don't you worry about chores, I got this." He put on his hat and when he noticed she wasn't moving, he tapped his toe exaggeratedly. "Quick, before my offer expires."

Emma crawled out of bed and arranged her body in the cleanest clothes she could find. Ten minutes later, she was buckling herself into Noah's truck. She sank down in the seat, wrapping her arms around her waist.

"Here." Noah handed her a pair of sunglasses from the dash and she slipped them over her eyes. The relief was immediate. "When's the last time you got loaded, anyways?"

"I don't know...like, maybe at Carter's wedding?"

"Em, that was four years ago."

"Ugh." She sank lower into the seat.

The drive to Hinkley's was short and her stomach was roaring when they opened the door and the smell of bacon hit her nose.

"Hey guys!" The diner's longest tenured

waitress, Tina, greeted them before she looked up. Emma had worked at Hinkley's after high school as a means for money for entry fees and had worked alongside the single mother for most of it. When she saw Emma, the redhead came around the counter and gave the younger girl a squeeze. "Oh, Emma, I heard you were back in town. I hope you're coming back to help me."

Emma pushed the sunglasses up on her head but regretted it—picture windows lined two walls in the diner. She was beginning to feel like a vampire.

"Probably not, hun. But it's nice to see you."

"Aw, that's a shame. You guys take whatever seat you want, I'll be right with you. Coffee?"

"The biggest mug you've got for this girl." Noah interjected.

Tina nodded, winked knowingly at Emma. "Karaoke at Danny's, right?"

"Ugh," Emma replied again. She'd come in to more than a few Monday morning breakfast shifts just like this, and Tina must have recognized it right away.

Despite her queasy stomach, when Noah touched his fingers to the small of her back to guide her toward a booth, she felt a sizzle low in her belly. He pulled the shade on the window lining the booth before sitting opposite her and Emma's headache reduced from a riot to a small protest.

Tina appeared with a coffee pot and two

mugs, filling both to the brim. "I'll be back for your orders."

Emma opened the menu but didn't look at it. She knew exactly what she'd end up with. Hinkley's served breakfast all day and the line cook, Len, did the best bacon and eggs Emma ever had, even in Denver. They tasted like manna from Heaven when consumed with a hangover. She took the opportunity to look over the menu at Noah. He didn't look like a man who had been awakened in the middle of the night and then put in a morning's worth of work at two ranches. He looked up and caught her eyes and a smile crossed his handsome features. It felt like it was just for her, and it made her melt a little.

"What?"

"How are you not dead on your feet?"

"I've just got a little extra shot of happy having you around." He lifted his mug to his lips.

She'd heard him use that terminology—and it was always in reference to visits from the girls he was dating at the time. A little bullet of anxiety quickened her heart rate. She'd always prided herself in remembering everything when she'd had too much to drink, but what if she didn't?

It was bad enough she'd come onto him, pawing him in his own bed in the middle of the night, but had she stopped there? She could remember her face pressed against his chest, the heat of their bodies so tight together, and the hardness...*Oh God*.

Tina showed up, then, her order pad in

hand, and beamed at the pair of them. "What can I get for yas?"

When she hesitated, Noah ordered first. When Tina's hundred-watt smile turned to Emma, she stuttered. "T-the regular."

~

Emma's expression stopped Noah halfway through the mouthful of coffee he'd swallowed as Tina left. She looked like she'd just seen a ghost and she'd definitely checked out of the conversation in favor of whatever was inside of her head. Noah waved a hand in front of her eyes.

"Earth to Em?"

She swallowed hard and flicked her eyes to him with a look that bordered on terror. "Did we...? Did I...?" Her voice rose with panic.

"What? No. Jesus, Emma. You were three sheets to the wind." He couldn't help the smirk that tipped the corner of his lips. Despite his body's demands, he'd made good and sure she wouldn't have any *real* regrets—that little bit of embarrassment was kind of cute, though. He watched her try to collect herself when Tina came to take the orders, and when she left, he leaned close, his voice low and private. "Trust me, when it happens, you'll remember it."

She cleared her throat and blanched, sitting back with wide eyes.

He chuckled and took a swig of coffee, shaking his head. He could have just as easily been toying with her, and she should have known it, but there had been something between them the night before that extended beyond normal two-naked-people chemistry, and she felt it, too. It was the only logical explanation for his normally unflappable companion to look like she'd been terrorized by the paranormal.

He watched her mentally scramble to right herself, and she finally did, filling the silence that stretched out between them with chatter.

"So. Dane's wedding. Tell me about his fiancée. Mama and daddy seem to really like her."

"Ren is something else. Dane's crazy about her. So's half of Three Rivers." Relieved she'd caught her stride again, he smiled.

"Mama says she brings something by at least once a week."

"She grew up in the city but she's really taken to mama's old garden." He nodded. "She and her sister had a rough go before they got here. Speaking of her sister..."

"Kerri, right?"

"Right. She's been riding old Buckshot at a couple of the gymkhana nights. She took to riding like a fish to water and I've been giving her lessons on the barrels but when I mentioned you were back in town, she said she'd love it if you could come watch her ride."

Emma flushed a little.

"She even found a couple of old videos of you from State championships back in senior year."

She groaned and rubbed a hand over her

face. "I don't suppose you were responsible for helping her 'find' those videos?"

He ignored her question. Of course he'd given the tapes to Kerri. "She practically thinks you're a celebrity."

"She knows I'm not, right?"

Tina appeared with their breakfasts and refilled their coffee cups. Emma visibly relaxed as she tucked into her breakfast and Noah smiled. As far as everyone here was concerned, she *was* a bit of a celebrity. In high school rodeo and even after, for a local, she'd done well, standing opposite him in the women's division at every race they went to—right at the top. Then she'd gone on to work for an outfit and hit the radar of anyone even remotely involved with rodeo. Even if she was a groom and not a rider, by most standards she had 'made it'.

"I didn't do anything to discourage the notion."

Emma stopped with a mouthful of bacon and shook her head ruefully at him. "You've always been my biggest fan."

"Always will be." And it was true.

He dug into his breakfast and the quiet settled between them for a while, more comfortable than it had been since she'd come home. She was more receptive to their old friendship than he ever envisioned she would be, and he was grateful for it, even if he didn't quite understand it yet. He didn't deserve her trust or forgiveness, but he hoped he could earn back her friendship. Either way, he'd missed this way too much.

ELEVEN

"THERE'S THE BAYLOR sister!" Finn teased, turning from where he'd been leaning against the arena fence watching a teenage girl warming up a horse that Emma recognized as Buckshot. He caught her up under his arm and gave her a squeeze and she couldn't help the smile. Renegade Racing was *like* a family, but this was the real thing, and she missed it.

The whole family was there – Dane, Finn, Noah, Gage, and a young auburn haired woman she assumed was Ren. Even Rex, Dane's old dog, was sitting next to Gage, patiently waiting for the boy to notice that he'd brought a stick for him to throw.

"Don't you all have anything better to do than watch me give a riding lesson?" Emma laughed as she took the empty spot between Finn and the woman. The girl in the ring looked perfectly at home on Buckshot as she long trotted him first around the outside of the ring, and then in figure eights through the middle of the arena. She was methodical and quiet, and the horse responded well to her. Emma watched her for a moment and concluded this would be primarily a mission of increasing the girl's confidence at speed. There wasn't a thing wrong with her riding.

"Well, I told them the best girl barrel racer I knew was coming and everyone needed to see what the fuss was about." Dane teased, bumping her with his shoulder. "You haven't met Ren and Kerri yet, have you?"

Emma shook her head and offered her hand to the girl standing next to her.

"This is Ren Maddock, my bride-to-be. And the girl in the ring is her sister, Kerri."

"It's nice to meet you, Emma. Thanks for doing this. We've heard all about you." She nodded past Emma who turned her head to see Noah shrugging with a guilty smile.

"It's no problem." Emma rolled her eyes at Noah. "These guys are family, and you will be soon, too."

"A year ago, Kerri had no riding experience," Finn explained. "But she's a fast learner, and has a natural way with the horses."

"She takes me trail riding," Gage informed her. Dane ruffled his unruly mop of blonde hair affectionately and he emerged from where he'd been hanging back by Ren's leg when Emma winked at him.

"She does. And she's going to need a new horse, soon." Noah chimed in. "Her ability is going to exceed Buckshot's soon. We just want her to be ready."

"Right. So who's teaching her now?" Emma asked. When all three brothers raised their hands, and then Gage did, too, she laughed. It was all too familiar. She shook her head and rolled her eyes and turned to Ren.

"Don't worry, she'll turn out fine. Even with this crew," she nodded toward the row of brothers, and then stepped through the planks of the fence, into the arena. "I turned out okay."

"So she says," Finn added. She shot him a look that was the universal sign for 'shut up, Finn' and started across the sand footing toward Kerri. The girl pulled up when she saw Emma coming and lifted her hand in greeting.

"Hey."

"Hey," the girl replied.

Emma reached out and stroked Buckshot's neck, thinking of the gelding in his prime. He'd been a heck of a horse, and he still was, clearly teaching new riders with a patience and forgiveness that came with age. He was just a little slower than he once was.

"You have great, quiet hands. I'm Emma."

The girl's face lit up. "Kerri. Noah showed me a video of your High School Rodeo Championship run. It was *awesome*."

Emma blushed. That had been a long time ago, her first season with Alamo, while they'd still been figuring one another out, and they'd gotten a lot better after that. But it was the season she'd learned to trust herself, and her horse.

"Well, I'll help you out however I can, but it looks like the boys have done a pretty good job. Or you're a natural. Or a little bit of both. Why don't we do a few figure eights at a nice easy lope to get started? At the cross over, bring him back to a trot for a few strides and then pick up the other lead."

Kerri nodded and turned away, executing the exercise with little effort at all. Emma called out pointers and encouragement to her and was pleased to find that she was more than competent. She shouldn't have expected anything less knowing the Baylors. They were fine horsemen on top of just being plain old good people. They wouldn't have taught her anything unless they taught her everything.

She put the pair through their paces for about thirty minutes – until she could tell both the horse and rider were reaching the end of their energy reserves. The next time, they'd work a little longer to build up endurance.

The crowd at the fence slowly dissipated and by the time she instructed Kerri to circle the ring a few times at a loose-reined walk to cool down, the only one left was Noah. She could have seen that one coming a mile away. She'd felt his eyes on her during the entire lesson and at first, it had been difficult to ignore, but as she'd settled into an easy teaching banter with the girl, she'd all but forgotten about him for the first time since she'd arrived home. Too bad it wasn't that easy the rest of the time.

~

Noah could have watched Emma teaching Kerri forever. Dane and Ren headed into the house with Gage to get supper ready, Finn went to feed, and Noah still hung over the fence watching her, like a lovesick teenager. She had a way with people just like she had a way with horses, and it was almost mesmerizing to watch her explaining things to Kerri that he had tried over and over but couldn't find the words for.

She finished her instruction and walked alongside Kerri as she cooled Buckshot down, talking to the teen and reaching out to touch Buckshot's neck from time to time. When they rounded the large sand arena and pulled up in front of Noah, Kerri swung off. Emma felt the horse's chest and nodded.

"He's all cool and dry now, he should be fine to just untack and brush off and give him a flake of hay."

"Thanks Emma."

The adoration was more than clear in Kerri's eyes and he couldn't help but suspect he was mirroring the same thing in his own. The teen moseyed off with the gelding behind her, traveling with his head low, his ears forward, engaged with the girl the entire time. The girl and the horse had taken to one another when she'd first arrived and it reminded Noah a lot of Emma and Alamo.

Emma shook her head and leaned against

the fence. "They're some pair."

Noah nodded. "They work together pretty great. I just wish they'd met ten years ago. She's just getting started and he's ready to retire."

"You guys have lots of nice prospects in from Reicher every year."

"Yeah but she's not *quite* ready for something that green."

Emma tilted her head thoughtfully. "Alamo's not doing anything. He'd be a perfect 'in between' horse. Get her used to some speed with no funny stuff. Besides, he's just going to sit while I'm in Denver. I'll never have time to bring him along."

It was a gut punch. He knew she'd go back to Denver, but it didn't make these little reminders any less painful. Every time she mentioned it, the urge to make things right between them got more frantic.

"He's a hell of a horse. You sure you don't want him in Denver? Make a little pocket change?"

She raised a brow. "We'd get creamed."

"I bet you and Alamo could beat us right now."

"No way." She shook her head, slipping her hands into the back pockets of her jeans and resting her weight on her right leg. The way her hips shifted was incredibly sexy. He let out a breath. "We're both so out of shape; I bet we couldn't turn the third barrel."

"Bullshit." He straightened from the fence and turned to lean against it. She followed suit, mimicking his stance. They were looking at the

Baylor family home now, with his pickup parked out front. "I bet you'd leave us in the dust."

"What are you willing to wager?"

She laughed and it was the best sound he'd heard in a long time.

"If I'm wrong and I kick your ass, I'll hand over the keys to my truck for a week."

"And if you're right and *I* kick *your* ass?"

"One kiss."

He was stepping out on a limb here, and maybe he was getting a mile and a half ahead of himself when it came to winning her over, but if it was a bust, they could laugh it off and get one step closer to that casual, easy relationship they'd once shared. Of course, he hoped it wouldn't be a bust. He wondered what she'd taste like; he already had an idea what she'd feel like under his hands, full of wanting, and he imagined what it might take to get her back there—sober, this time.

Even though he hadn't gotten any closer, she took a step back. Her expression froze on her face—a smile that said she didn't know what was going on.

"What the hell, Noah?"

"Just trust me on this one." *Come on, now.* It took her a minute, but the girl he knew, the one who never missed a told-ya-so chance to hand him his ass on a platter finally surfaced. It was like he'd hit her restart button. He could tell by the way she straightened and one eyebrow snapped up in a challenge.

"I'm sure gonna enjoy your truck."

"I don't think so." Noah laughed. He reached across the space between them, offering his hand. She slid hers into it and he traced the tips of his fingers along the inside of her wrist, the erratic thread of her pulse bumping under them. He felt like a kid in the candy store.

"We'll see."

TWELVE

FEELING REJUVENATED AFTER a visit with Stephanie, Emma drove home, the route so familiar she could have done it with her eyes closed. It was just ten minutes but it gave her some time to consider her friend's words. They'd spent all afternoon over coffee while Emma tried to figure out where her head was. She'd been sure Noah's declaration two years ago was a means to keep her around so she could continue to enable his lifestyle. Nothing would ever develop between them, he'd turned that horse out to pasture when Gavin died, and he started blatantly picking up girls who couldn't have been more physically different than she was. And then he'd thrown a wrench into her entire plan for self-preservation with that stupid bet two days ago. He hadn't mentioned it again and she had half convinced herself he'd forgotten about it.

Stephanie had done her best to untangle the list of 'friend stuff' versus 'not-just-friend stuff' that Emma had composed, but at the end of the day, she'd given up and declared that Emma probably already knew exactly what she needed to do.

Up until leaving for Denver, she'd never done anything but meet a challenge head-on. Noah made her trip up. She'd run instead of resolving issues with him before she left, and now she was clinging desperately to her belief that he was a bad person in order to protect herself. And it wasn't fair to anyone. They needed to talk.

Pulling into the driveway, she saw him sitting on the corral fence with Alamo, saddled up and ready to go. He slid down when he saw her car, that signature shit-eating grin on his face. He was up to something.

She parked and got out, her brow furrowed.

"What do you think you're doing?" Approaching, she spoke low to the horse and slid a hand down his glossy neck; Noah hadn't done a half bad job grooming.

"Time to put your money where your mouth is." A little thrill of excitement jack-knifed through her at his words, and she struggled to contain it.

"Hey, it's *your* money." *But our mouths.* "You started..."

Noah silenced her with a hand in the air.

"Get on." He gestured to Alamo.

"I don't..."

"Did you go soft in Denver?"

"What?" She frowned.

"Well the Emma I knew before she went to Denver didn't back down from anything, least of all a bet. Especially if it meant she'd be right about something." He teased. "You never pass up a chance to have the last word."

Scowling, she knew he was right. She glowered at him and screwed her ball cap down on her head. Putting a foot in the stirrup, she levered herself onto Alamo's back and Noah handed her the reins. Together, they crossed the property line, skirting between the fence and a bush and found themselves on the Baylor property. They approached the long outdoor riding arena on the other side of the driveway and Noah opened the gate for her, patting her knee as she rode by. Her body reacted with a tiny tremor. Before her conversation with Stephanie, she might not have even noticed the casual touch. Now, it set her on fire.

Emma narrowed her eyes at the cloverleaf pattern of barrels set out before her and let out a breath, hoping to calm the butterflies fluttering low in her belly. Beneath her, Alamo released a bored sigh.

This was a losing bet. She knew it when she shook Noah's hand. He was still actively competing on the circuit and she'd spent as much time on horseback total since coming home from Denver as Noah did on an average day. It was sweet of him to try to bolster her confidence by insisting she would beat him, but there was no way it would happen. She would try. Of course, she would try. Because maybe she *wanted* to lose the bet. Thinking of losing and Noah kissing her made those butterflies flare up again.

"Time's a wastin', sweetheart." Noah leaned against one of the corral posts, a stopwatch in hand. He had insisted that he wouldn't get his horse until she had run her pattern, and she was just about certain he was up to something. She lifted her sunglasses and squinted at him across the arena.

"I'm just preparing myself for defeat."

"Come on, you were the hottest thing on a horse for most of your high school career and Alamo couldn't be beat. He could do this without you and *still* kick my ass."

Emma blushed. It was true—she had been at the top until she had backed down to work full time to save to get out of Three Rivers. Rodeo money wasn't consistent and she wasn't a patient woman.

"Maybe three years ago..."

Noah shushed her and lifted the stopwatch into the air. "Enough of your pity party. Ride the pattern."

It was as if they'd never taken a break as she circled Alamo twice. He was just waiting for her cue to begin the pattern. One thing that made him stand out in a crowd of barrel racers was the fact that he was hardly interested in the pattern until his rider turned him to it. Over his years in competition, Alamo had seen lots of things besides the barrels and so, unlike many of the top contenders who were barely controllable once they entered the ring, he stood quietly, the perfect gentleman, waiting for her cue.

Taking a deep breath, Emma leaned forward and prepared for the horse's rocket-ship launch. She squeezed lightly and kissed under her breath and Alamo dug in, shooting toward the barrels at a speed that nearly knocked her out of the saddle. He turned deep and tight around each barrel with hardly any guidance from his rider and when he rounded the third one, kicked it into another gear that brought a trill of laughter out of Emma. She pulled him up at the end of the arena with a smile nearly eating up her face to the sound of Noah whooping.

He threw the stopwatch into the air and crossed the arena in three long strides. "Holy shit, girl! That was impressive! You could still race the circuit in the money like that."

Emma flushed with pleasure and gave Alamo a pat on the neck. She had been standing on the sidelines, watching someone else enjoy the rush of the pattern for the last two years, and had forgotten how thrilling it could be.

"Alright, cowboy, don't get too excited. I still want to see *your* time."

He nodded and took off for the barn while she dismounted and retrieved the stopwatch from the sand. Leading Alamo out of the ring, she climbed back through the fence and held his reins through the slats. When she saw Noah emerging from the barn with Buckshot, she shook her head. The horse could turn it on...to about halfway. His potential topped out about where horses like Blackjack and Alamo decided to stop messing around and fire up the engines. Sure, he was in shape, but he just didn't have the motor the two younger horses had.

"What the hell, Noah?"

"Kerri has been using Buckshot at gymkhanas," he said, defensively.

"Buckshot is a thousand years old."

He held up his hand to silence her, shaking his head. "The bet in no way, shape, or form specified which horse I would be riding to try to beat your time."

Narrowing her eyes, she tipped her head at him but waved her hand to allow it. On the outside, she worked hard to maintain the most casual expression, but her heart thundered in her throat and her mouth was dry as sandpaper. She knew there was no way Buckshot could beat Alamo, even if Noah juiced every ounce of power out of the horse, and he wasn't that kind of horseman. He was going to kiss her. And she was going to let him.

She watched him mount up effortlessly, swinging a long leg over the horse's back. Noah's feet dangled below Buckshot's belly; he was much too tall for the child's mount. Even so, the man looked completely natural astride and it was like a punch in her gut. Far from the glitz and glam of the professional racing outfit she'd been working for, she'd forgotten what a true horseman looked like astride.

"It doesn't count if you ride the pattern

backwards, Baylor!" She called to him, watching as he trotted a couple of circles, loosening up Buckshot's muscles.

He paused, winked at her, and turned the horse toward the barrels. She started the stopwatch as he rode past her, still trotting. She waited for him to increase his speed but the horse seemed perfectly content to plod along at a speed just barely beyond a walk. Emma groaned, leaned back against the rail fence and rolled her eyes, watching him take a snail's pace through a course she knew Blackjack could accomplish in a fraction of the time that Buckshot was taking.

Noah pulled up near her, looking entirely too proud of himself. Emma let out the breath she realized that she'd been holding as he dismounted and swung the reins down off of Buckshot's neck. The butterflies were back. He'd skewed the playing field to ensure he would win the bet. And winning the bet meant he kissed her. And skewing the playing field meant he *wanted* to kiss her. Her heart shot off the way Alamo had for the first barrel, and she could barely keep up.

Buckshot followed Noah as he stalked toward her, the playfulness in his eyes replaced by the same expression she'd seen in the barn that first night. She swallowed hard, pressing her back against the fence, simultaneously wishing she could disappear and wondering what was taking him so damn long to get to her.

"That's not fair..." Her halfhearted protest was cut off when he got to her, tipped her ball cap back, and lifted her chin with two fingers.

"The only rule was that you had to beat me." His voice was tight and low. Heat simmered deep in the pit of her belly, the giddy feeling gone and replaced with a persuasive desire. This *definitely* didn't belong on the 'friend stuff' list. "And now I'm going to collect my winnings."

He dropped Buckshot's reins and used his free hand to draw the ball cap off of her head, releasing her loose ponytail and spilling hair over her bare shoulders. More than anything, she wanted to look away from his intense gaze but she tipped her head down and held it defiantly. She'd lost the bet—he hadn't played fair, but she had lost, and she wouldn't back down.

One corner of his lips tipped up, amused and he bent his head, his mouth hovering over hers for a beat. Alamo's reins slid out of her fingers.

"Breathe, Em."

She hadn't realized she'd been holding it until he dropped his lips to the base of her throat and she released it in a hot rush. Without realizing what she was doing, she tipped her head to the side, inviting the gentle caress of his mouth on her flesh. It felt like sin and she wasn't ready for redemption.

They'd gotten this close once, the summer before Gavin's accident. During hay season, they'd been ranking bales in the loft and he'd wrestled her to the ground and given her a good burn on her neck with his stubble. It had been light, and playful. This was decidedly not.

His lips swept to the soft spot behind her

ear and then along her jaw and she shifted her body closer to his, her fingers curling in the fabric of his shirt at his waist. It was so much more than just a kiss. It was a tempting seduction, a declaration of intent. He didn't want to just blow a raspberry on her lips in jest; he wanted to love on her. The realization made her pull him closer.

Noah slid a hand under her hair and cupped her neck, tipping her head back and opening her to him. A soft noise escaped her with her next breath. Emma's heart thundered in her chest, her mind void of anything except for the masterful way he claimed her mouth. She drew him closer still; their bodies cinched together, his weight pressing her into the boards of the fence. The kiss was firm and confident, the taste of him a relief after the last week. He kissed her like he knew how she liked to be kissed, which was impossible but made complete sense all at once. She could have settled in and lived in the moment, with the adrenaline of the barrel pattern still thrumming through her veins heated by fiery desire he incited.

"Hey, Alamo was wandering home..." Finn's voice startled Emma so badly she jerked away, biting down on Noah's lip in the process. Not in the sexy way. *Shit*. Noah cussed as Emma spun around to see Noah's middle brother leading her horse back across the yard, a knowing smile spread across his features. Damn these Baylor men. They thought they knew everything and they were usually right.

She frowned and opened the gate of the

arena, taking the reins from Finn.

"Thanks...mama and daddy would have panicked when he came home without me."

She couldn't make eye contact with either of them. She'd spent most of her childhood catching frogs and playing hide and seek, then hitching rides to rodeo events and sitting around campfires with both of them and now the easy camaraderie was spoiled by desire she thought she'd put to bed. Any inkling of *want* she had stuffed in the back of her closet for Noah her entire life had been ignited like dry kindling and she was spitting mad.

"Anyways, I should go." Without lifting her eyes, she put her hand on the horn and cantle of the saddle and mounted up. "Thanks for the challenge, Noah. See you later, Finn." Without another word, she put her heels to Alamo and trotted away before she said—or did—something she regretted.

THIRTEEN

SWEET JESUS. NOAH let out a careful breath as he watched Emma trot out of the yard. The taste of her lingered on his lips and already he wanted more. He hadn't expected to be so affected by the kiss. It was all he could do to stop himself from following her right down to her daddy's front step and doing it all over again. How the hell had he danced around something so addictive for so long?

She'd always been there, barely a hundred yards from his front door, and today that felt too far. He clucked his tongue and turned as Buckshot nudged his back pocket looking for treats.

He'd been so caught up, he'd nearly forgotten about Finn, who he found watching him with a raised brow and his arms crossed over his broad chest.

"Buckshot? Seriously?"

"I bet her she'd win and I knew there was no way I could slow Blackjack down enough." Noah shrugged and gathered up Buckshot's reins, patting the old horse on the neck. "Old Buckshot was my insurance policy."

"I see." Finn's expression was unreadable.

"She was pretty damn good. Even if I *hadn't* been riding the oldest horse in the barn, she might have beaten me."

"Sure." Finn stepped back and opened the gate for Noah and Buckshot to pass through.

"With a couple of months of conditioning." Noah grinned, heading for the barn with the horse following obediently behind.

Finn shook his head. "Well, whatever is going on there...just be careful."

Noah swung his gaze to his brother.

"Emma Pierce is a sweet girl and she doesn't deserve to get the runaround. You be straight with her. Maybe she wants to be your passing fancy, but make it clear that's all it is."

"I appreciate what you're trying to do here, but it's none of your damn business." Noah's little high sucked right out of him at Finn's admonishment. He knew he'd invited Finn to this conversation the other day after Emma hadn't let him apologize, but that didn't mean he wanted the intervention, now. Not while his blood still ran warm from the feel of her under his hands.

Finn bristled. "It'll be none of my damn business anymore when I feel absolutely sure I'm not gonna have to answer a call from Banks at 3am and pull you out of the drunk tank. Or drive some heartbroken little girl home when you've locked her out of your bedroom. Or to the hospital when you won't answer the phone."

Noah's heart tripped a little. He knew Finn doubted him, it would have been hard not to, considering the messes he had to clean up after Emma left. And every once in a while, Finn liked to push his buttons, to test him. Noah recognized that in Finn's words now, but it didn't make him any less pissed off to have his mistakes thrown back in his face all the time.

He'd never wanted to hit his brother so badly, but Noah kept himself in check. Jaw clenched, he let a tight breath out through his nose. There had been times when Finn had shown him mercy and kindness when he didn't deserve it and though he didn't think his brother was particularly deserving today, his balled fists remained at his sides, his knuckles aching to connect with Finn's jaw. Sure, Finn had given him a poke or two and Noah had never fought back...but for Emma, he was willing to.

When he didn't reply, Finn scuffed his boots against the gravel in the yard. "Don't you hurt that girl, Noah."

As quickly as he'd appeared, Finn left, turning for his cabin behind the big house.

"Damnit." Noah cursed quietly, picked up Buckshot's reins and led him to the barn. It had taken him a good long while to figure it out, especially when he'd been more drunk than sober, but he wanted Emma; mind, body and soul. It was more obvious now than it had ever been.

FOURTEEN

EMMA HEARD HER mother call her name from the bottom of the stairs and did one last quick check in the mirror. She passed her hands over her waist, rendered smooth and tight by the most inhumane pair of underwear invented. They weren't sexy but they gave her the illusion of ten pounds less, which, in the grand scheme of things didn't amount to much, but made her feel better.

Her heart skipped a beat as she thought of being Noah's date tonight. She hadn't seen him since she'd ridden away from the Baylor property yesterday, her body full of wanting. He'd been busy this morning with preparations for the wedding and she'd done the feeding herself, with her dad's company. The memory of him touching her kept a low grade dose of desire running through her veins and she was more excited to see him tonight than she cared to admit.

Releasing a nervous breath, she left her

room and started down the stairs. Her stomach performed anxious flip-flops. *Traitor.* She didn't want to be this invested but she couldn't help herself.

Her parents waited at the bottom, and her father scooped her up with his good arm and pressed a kiss to the top of her head. "You look lovely, sweetie."

"Thanks, Daddy."

The trio departed the house, taking the short cut across the yard. The ranch had been transformed. The decorative post and rail fence running up the drive was strung in delicate white lights. A huge white tent with a peaked roof had been erected, and in the waning day, light and the noise of merriment spilled out onto the grass. Judging by the lineup of cars in the yard and people milling about outside, the whole town was there.

She recognized Noah's figure standing outside the door of the tent well before he noticed her, and she took a moment to savor it. For the first time in days, she felt like she might have the upper hand.

He made a fine silhouette in a crisp white shirt tucked into dark, fitted jeans. He wore a navy vest that stretched tight across his shoulders and tapered at the waist, and was fidgeting with a black felt cowboy hat in his hands. When he looked up and caught sight of her, she drew in a breath. Even though she was flanked by her parents, she felt like the only other person on the Baylor property. A broad smile broke over his handsome face and everything inside of her heated up a few degrees.

"Looking good, Em." She rolled her eyes and he turned his attention to her mother but his eyes lingered a second after he turned his head. "And you are lovely as ever, Myrna. Jonas." He shook her father's hand. "Go on in, the party is just getting started."

Her parents headed into the tent and Emma moved to follow them but he caught her elbow, holding her back. Her skin tingled where his calloused fingers touched her, and the closeness took the breath out of her.

He ducked his head, his mouth so close to her ear she could feel his hot, damp breath. "I mean it."

She felt the blush creep up her neck and stain her cheeks and was glad that the light was dim when he drew back. She lifted her gaze to his, with her heart rattling around in her throat like a snare drum.

"You don't clean up half bad yourself." The words were meant to be a tease, but she missed the mark because of the fire his touch put in her veins, and they came out flat.

With a slanted half smile that made her weak in the knees, he released her, but moved his hand to the small of her back and guided her toward the door of the tent. They passed through a throng of bodies and headed straight toward the bar where Cutter Anderson was serving up drinks. A huge chalkboard sign said '*Have a drink and settle in. By the end of the night, we'll all be kin.*'.

"Emma Pierce, are you ever a sight for sore eyes."

Emma blushed and waved her hand at Cutter dismissively. "Don't give me a hard time, Cutter, just give me a double spiced rum and Coke."

The bartender winked and flipped the spirits bottle over a rock glass, making a drink that ended up being only about a third cola.

"Be careful with that rot-gut, Em. I don't wanna be scraping you up off the dance floor later on." His tone was teasing and it took her back a few years. She'd gone on a few dates with Cutter after graduation, but nothing had ever come of it. They'd had a great time together, cracking each other up with jokes and teasing, but nobody had ever stuck like Noah.

"At least the drive home isn't that far this time," Noah said, winking at her.

"I'll be back...on my own two feet." She laughed and tipped her glass at Cutter. The bartender slid a bottle of beer across the bar to Noah.

"*Hey*!" Emma would have recognized Caine Baylor's deep baritone anywhere, and she turned her head to find him standing on a chair near the front of the tent. "It's time for you folks to take your seats, my son's about to get hitched."

He swept his arm to the outside of the tent where rows of straw bales had been laid out with burlap covers on either side of an aisle. At the front, a delicate white archway was heavy with an assortment of flowers, and Banks Montgomery stood, waiting. What wasn't backlit by a spectacular mountain sunset was illuminated by tea lights in mason jars. Noah touched her elbow again.

"Groomsmen are terrible dates. Call me selfish, but I didn't want to risk someone else snapping you up." He pressed a kiss to her cheek that felt anything but casual. "I'll be back, I promise."

She watched him go with a bemused smile and then, with her drink in hand, found her parents in the crowd. They filed toward the rows of seats, settling comfortably amongst the rest of the guests. The sign by the bar had more truth to it than she had realized, as she noticed faces she recognized and loved, right down to Mrs. Bates in her motor scooter. The elderly woman had a rock glass in hand and it almost made Emma laugh out loud. Mrs. Bates could be a menace *without* adding alcohol to the mix.

Emma's heart seized a little when she saw Dane and his two brothers file down the aisle and assemble at the front. In matching dark cowboy hats, jeans and vests, they looked so grown up—a far cry from the boys she'd known in her childhood. She was proud and touched and happy she'd ended up home, if it was for this moment, alone. Her nostalgic reverie was broken when Noah targeted her out of the crowd and winked, making her stomach flip. *Damnit.*

Before long, Gage and Kerri started up the aisle, hand in hand. The little boy was dressed similar to the men at the front, and carried a barn board sign that said "*Uncle Dane, here comes your girl!*" Emma remembered all too well the accident that had shaken the small, tight knit town when Gage's parents had been killed. She'd sat long hours with her mother in the Baylor kitchen while Myrna helped Dane go through the paperwork to take legal guardianship of his nephew, as Gavin had requested in his will. It had been a difficult time for everyone, but the giant smile and clear adoration in the young boy's eyes as he looked at his uncle told her the transition had gone smoothly in the last two years.

The pair assembled themselves on the bride's side of the aisle. It was clear they had a special relationship as Gage looked up at her and she leaned to whisper something to him, and then point down the aisle as the music changed and everyone rose.

Escorted by Caine, Ren started down the aisle in a beautiful lace gown with capped sleeves and a bouquet of wildflowers. Myrna grasped Emma's arm as tears began to well up in her eyes. Something about weddings always did it to her; the best part, above all else was the earnest expression of love on Ren's face. She looked like she was barely restraining herself from running down the aisle to Dane. Emma glanced quickly at him at the front; he was barely keeping it together, his eyes locked on his approaching fiancée. The guests seemed to let out a collective happy sigh when they finally made it to one another and joined hands.

"You can be seated," Banks said. Emma

noted that he had no papers to read from. He clasped his hands together, his voice carrying over the group. "On behalf of Ren and Dane and Caine and Ella, I'd like to thank you for being here. We're thrilled to have you here to witness us officially welcoming Ren and Kerri into this family. I think you all know how important these two women are to the community and we couldn't be more thankful that they found us when they did.

"If there's anybody here who can think of a reason why these two soulmates shouldn't be together, you better get your backside out of here on threat of being hauled down to my office afterwards." A ripple of chuckles moved through the crowd but everyone stayed seated and quiet, and Banks continued, mentioning remembrance of Ren's father and Gavin.

"We know that what we're doing here today would make them happy. It's also the wish of Caine and Ella Baylor that Ren and Kerri are welcomed into the family as daughters and sisters. Now, for the good stuff."

Banks turned to Dane and Ren.

"Do you both come here of your own free will to be joined together as husband and wife, partners in the walk of life?"

"We do," the couple replied.

"Then I'll let you two do the talking."

Emma held her breath when Ren began speaking. She didn't know the woman well, but the emotion in her trembling voice was enough to bring tears to every eye in the crowd. Emma's mother clutched her arm.

"I sincerely believed this journey through life was mine to walk alone. Then I met you and found someone to hold my hand and walk beside me, support me when I was weak, and carry me when I couldn't take another step. You have been my friend and my protector, my refuge in stormy weather. I couldn't ask for someone with more patience, more understanding, more love, or more kindness than you.

"I promise everything that I am and have to you, today. To be the partner to you that you have been to me. To hold your hand and walk beside *you*, support *you* when you are weak, and carry *you* when you can't take another step. Through all of the goodness and the misfortune that life may pass our way, I promise to be your friend, your lover, your confidante—until the end of my days."

Dane lifted their joined hands and brushed his lips over her knuckles, never taking his eyes off of hers.

"You came into my life at a time when I didn't even know how badly I needed you, and lifted me up in ways I'd never imagined I wanted. I've never felt more like myself than I do when I'm with you. You're an amazing woman; I'm so blessed to share my life with you, and you're my best friend." Dane's voice hitched with emotion and he stopped a moment, clearing his throat. There wasn't a dry eye in the group of guests.

"I promise to give the best of myself to you and never ask you for more than you can give, to stand with you when things go the way we plan and when they don't. I promise to love all of you with faithfulness and honesty and gentleness that you deserve. Until I take my dying breath, every part of me will love every part of you."

When Emma looked up, with her eyes full of tears and her bare arms covered in goose bumps, Noah made eye contact, holding her gaze for a loaded moment. It only broke when her mother touched her arm and handed her a tissue.

Banks moved through the other traditional parts of the ceremony and all too soon, Dane dipped Ren back and sealed the deal with a kiss. The newlyweds raised their joined hands triumphantly, leading the wedding party down the aisle and straight toward the bar. All of the guests were on their feet, surging toward the tent to follow the processional, and Emma found herself swept up with them, her heart near to bursting.

FIFTEEN

NOAH SHIFTED FOOT to foot as the receiving line came through. Gage tugged on his pant leg, wedged between his uncle and Kerri to keep him entertained, but Noah couldn't stop scanning the crowd for Emma. He was happy to stand for his brother but he'd had a hell of a time keeping his eyes off her during the ceremony. All of a sudden, he felt like he was seventeen years old and horny for his prom date again.

The dress she wore drove him near to distraction. It was simple; a blush pink with short sleeves and a scoop neck but it hugged her body in all the right places and the way it hung off of her curvaceous hips just about made his knees weak. Her long hair hung in loose curls over her shoulders, reaching nearly to mid back. She'd always kept it long but she was doing something different with it now, something more grown up. Every time he'd seen her since she'd come home, she seemed more like a woman and less like the girl he had grown up with. The kiss yesterday had done nothing to dissuade that.

Finally, he saw her making her way up the line, between her mother and father. He was happy to have been a part of his brother's happiness but he wished he'd had a chance to talk to her about losing the bet. Something had changed in that moment. Sure, he'd wanted her since she'd left for Denver. But the kiss, the way she responded, made him think for the first time that maybe he could have her. Maybe she wanted him, too. Maybe they wouldn't be resigned to a life of awkwardness, her in Denver and him here wishing she'd just come home.

A sweet, gentle blush flushed her cheeks as she got closer in the line, hugging first Finn, then Kerri, then Gage, and then finally arriving in front of him. She'd seen him looking, clearly. This was a new side to Emma that he'd never seen before. A little nervous, a little flattered. It was endearing. She stepped into his arms easily, and he dropped a hand to her back and pressed her body to his for just a beat, a little tighter than anyone else. The flush had deepened when he let her go and he smiled, then turned to address both her and her mother.

"Both of you ladies better save a dance for me." Then he glanced at Jonas and laughed. "If Jonas here'll permit it, I guess."

Jonas Pierce let loose a belly laugh. He was a good man—like a second father—and he had been all too happy to help him when he had needed it. Lord knew he'd supported Noah when he needed it. Borrow his tractor? That's just fine. Borrow his daughter? Might be a bit trickier. *Best to ease him in.*

"Of course. One apiece. Better make it a good one," Jonas said as he passed by, shaking Noah's hand and moving on to the newlyweds. Myrna ushered Emma along but she gave him one hell of a long look before she passed.

The next hour went by in a blur, as the rest of the guests filed by, dinner was served and Dane and Ren took to the floor for their first dance. Caine surprised her with a father-daughter dance. Noah sat at the head table, watching, toasted when he should, and gave a speech welcoming Ren and Kerri to their family, but he never lost tabs on Emma. She had nearly as many people chatting with her as the bride and groom when people who hadn't seen her for two years noticed her presence. He was pretty sure they'd just sent an open invitation to the whole town and everyone had shown up.

Once all of the traditionally required dances were finished, Noah finally had a moment to seek her out in the crowd again. She was tangled up in conversation with Mrs. Bates. The elderly woman had a hell of a time keeping the Baylor boys straight in her mind but seemed to recognize Emma. He shook a few hands and received a few hugs on the route across the busy dance floor but the thought of taking her in his arms for a dance drew him through the crowd like a magnet.

Reaching her, he touched her elbow gently.

"Mrs. Bates, I hate to interrupt, but I'm going to steal Emma away for a dance."

Emma raised a brow in his direction but said nothing.

"Alright, Gavin." Mrs. Bates responded, bestowing the sweetest smile on him. "You be good to that girl."

"You're next." He winked at the older woman without bothering to correct her, and turned Emma toward the dance floor.

She shook her head. "That must be tough."

"She means well, she just gets confused." He paused a moment to gather himself. Mrs. Bates *did* mean well, but her confusion could be painful. Clearing his throat, he straightened his shoulders. Not long ago, he'd have gone straight to the bar and not stopped until his heart stopped hurting. Now he had something else to soothe the ache for a little while.

Emma gave him a long look before he moved one hand to the small of her back and guided her to the middle of the dance floor. A slow country song flooded the speakers. The floor was crowded with people who, following the last fast song, had sorted themselves into partners—some of them belonged to one another, others were new pairings.

He turned Emma into his arms easily, putting one hand on her hip and watching as their hands came together in the most natural way, hers—smaller, softer—closed in his fingers. She fit perfectly, though he knew there had been times when she'd felt like she didn't fit any place at all. She slid her palm up his arm and came to rest grasping his shoulder. Her face lifted and she flashed him a smile that made his heart race.

They stood at a distance that was entirely too formal for the way his blood heated at the spots where they touched, and he moved his hand from her hip to the small of her back, bringing her just a bit closer. Close enough that their bodies found new points to touch, their temples tipped toward one another, cheeks a fraction of an inch apart. So close he could feel the heat between them and wanted to crawl inside of it and die happy.

His heart settled, right where it was meant to be. Slowly, they moved, hips swaying, bodies in sync, the way they had been for years and years. She was right where she belonged, by his estimation. She just didn't know it yet.

The music, the crowd, the night itself faded away as he held her, their movements slow and relaxed. They were so comfortable it didn't matter who else saw, and they melted into one another. He tucked their joined hands against his chest and she opened her palm over his heart; he covered it with his own. A slow, hot breath breezed past his ear and her hand slid a bit higher on his shoulder, her warm fingers stroking the hairs at the nape of his neck. They didn't need a single word.

Just being with her set him at ease. He'd painstakingly put all the pieces of his life together while she'd been gone, but had always felt like there was something missing. And here it was, right in his arms. Jonas had said to make their one dance a good one and he couldn't think of anything better.

She looked like she was just about to put her head to his chest when he felt a tap on his shoulder and turned to see Finn. He held out a hand for Emma and like that, she stepped out of his arms and into his brother's, leaving Noah feeling cold and out of place. It was the second time in as many days that he might have taken a swing at Finn, but tonight, more than yesterday, he recognized that his brother's protectiveness was for Emma's benefit and not Noah's punishment.

He left the dance floor reluctantly, looking over his shoulder once to see Emma's eyes open, her hands where it was appropriate. Finn appeared to be teasing her, and she was smiling, and though he knew there was no competition between he and his brother, Noah felt a pang of jealousy. He arrived at the bar a second later.

Cutter lifted a beer bottle to the counter top and cracked the top for Noah, without taking an order. Had he not already opened the beer, Noah might have gone for something a little harder. It would have been a bad idea. Cutter had his back, and he was grateful for that.

He nodded his thanks to the bartender, but his eyes quickly found Emma in the crowd again, turning with Finn, and he settled with his elbow on the bar to watch her. She was tipping her head back and laughing now. She looked happy, and it made him happy.

"You've got it bad," Cutter said behind him.

Noah twisted to look at the other man, raising a brow. He knew Emma took issue with the rumor mill that ran the town and he needed to protect this little spark they were fostering.

"It's Emma," Noah said. As if that was explanation enough.

"Exactly. It's Emma." Cutter shook his head, sliding a couple of empties off of the bar and into a waiting bin. "She's always been your weak spot, man."

Noah had a lot of weak spots, if one was keeping count. Though he hated to hear the words, he knew Cutter was right about this one. When he didn't reply, the bartender continued.

"I was shocked as hell you never went to Denver to bring her back, actually."

"You and the rest of Three Rivers, apparently."

Noah tipped the beer to his lips as the song ended and Finn finally released Emma. He saw the sheriff snag her as she passed by. He said something funny and she laughed, then looked toward Noah—she hadn't been as obvious, but she'd kept track of him the entire time, too.

SIXTEEN

EMMA STEPPED AWAY from Banks and slipped out of the tent. It was warm inside and she was still overwhelmed by the way her body responded in Noah's arms. Sure, Finn and Banks distracted her from it for a minute, but the heat from his gaze across the tent reminded her of the way her mouth went dry when she'd put her hand over his heart and felt it thudding, as if it was just for her.

She needed a minute to collect herself. The plan had been to come home and help her father get the ranch in order while he healed, not to come home and fall into the abyss of loving Noah. She had to get her head on straight—she couldn't be in Denver for the rest of her contract both homesick and wanting him, especially if it wasn't reciprocated. It was a dangerous cycle to get caught in and she couldn't move forward if her heart stayed back here in Three Rivers.

The cool night air hit her bare arms and she

rubbed her palms over her biceps in an attempt to warm them. She should have brought a sweater but she hadn't thought that far ahead. She'd been too excited to get here and see him. Her heart told her she was in a whole mess of trouble, and she'd do best not to forget that.

Apart from the raucous party going on inside of the tent, the Baylor ranch was quiet. She'd spent more than a few nights racing through the yard in the dark, playing hide and seek past her bedtime on summer nights that felt endless. In truth, the Baylor spread felt like an extension of her home next door. It was different to come back to it after two years, but it felt as comfortable as it always had.

A plaid blanket dropped over her shoulders, startling her.

"They set them out there for a reason, you know," Noah teased. The deep timbre of his voice so close at her back made the tiny hairs on her nape stand up. She resisted the urge to take a step back, let him put his arms around her, feel the warmth of his body, and instead turned to offer him a smile.

"Shouldn't you be tending to your duties as a groomsman?" She tried to keep the mood light but he was still standing so close they shared the air they breathed.

He waved his hand dismissively. "Finn's got things under control. I saw you step out and thought I'd make sure you were okay."

A smile lifted her lips and she tugged the blanket around her arms, wrapping herself up. If she was busy holding the blanket, maybe she wouldn't be tempted to let her heart talk her into stepping into the space between them and doing something she might regret.

"Always looking out for me."

He reached out and rubbed his hands over the blanket on her biceps and almost without her realizing it, eased her into his warm embrace. Her fisted fingers were caught up between them, wound into the edges of the blanket and she opened them up, pressing her palms flat against his broad chest. She could feel his heart beating a slow, steady thrum under the heels of her hands. Constant, like his presence in her life. Even when she'd been in Denver, even when she'd been angry at him, even when she'd found brief respite in someone else's bed, Noah was there.

He was, at the same time, completely different from the Noah she'd known before and exactly the same. It was appealing and exciting and it was part of what had drawn her to him time and time again since she'd come home.

She nestled against his body heat, tucking her head under his chin, and let out a sigh. It was the closest she had been to anybody in two years. It felt right. Her heart was winning this battle without a doubt. She squeezed her eyes shut and wished she could resist, even if it was only for the sake of making her contract easier to finish. And then she realized she didn't want to resist, and she wasn't fooling anyone, not even herself.

She felt him swallow.

"Em, I've been trying to figure out the right words since you got out of your car in your daddy's yard."

Her heart almost stopped when he started speaking and she waited a moment before she lifted her head and met his eyes, searching. They were clear as a bell—he'd had a few drinks, but no more than she had, and this wasn't like the last time. He kept her held close, an insurance policy.

"There's nothing I can say that can take us right back to the beginning, I know that. You'll always have the leftover hurt from the way I treated you before you left." He loosened his grip with one hand and traced his thumb over her cheekbone, his dark eyes remorseful. "And I know there's nothing I can do to erase that. But I'd spend my whole life trying to, if you'd let me."

Her heart started beating again, an industrial jackhammer now, right at the base of her throat.

"Noah..."

"I've made a lot of mistakes. And a lot of them hurt you, betrayed our friendship, and damaged what we could have had."

What we could have had. She let out a breath through her nose. If he hadn't been holding her, she might have run, but there was something comforting in his embrace, in his words.

"I'm sorry, Em. And I know I don't deserve for you to forgive me, and I can't expect for things to go back the way they were."

She wriggled a hand out from between

their bodies and touched his cheek.

"We don't have to do this right now." She knew she was skirting around the issue again, but the night so far had been too magical, too enticing, too comfortable to mangle it with the hard conversation she knew they would eventually have to have. She wanted to get back into that warmth they'd had between them on the dance floor. "Let's just have tonight. We have time."

~

"Emma..."

"Noah." The caress of her voice on his name felt as good as she did in his arms. He hadn't expected her to stop him, and at the same time, he hadn't expected her to let him get this far. And then, even better, with a short breath that told him she'd bet all her chips on this move, slid her hand across his jaw, to the back of his neck and drew his mouth down to hers. She touched her lips to his tentatively, and pulled back when it took him a second to respond. He hadn't expected this. Hurt registered in her eyes for just a beat before he tugged her to him, tight.

Not for the first time, he thought that if she had stayed, he might have taken a different path. But she'd needed to leave, for herself, and for him.

Her absence and Finn's prompting had driven him to be a better man, better than the one he'd been before. If she'd stayed, he might never have changed. He might have hurt her worse than he had. With her gone, he measured himself against the type of man that someone like Emma deserved. He didn't know if he was there now, but he hoped to God he was.

A couple of girls came out of the tent hand-in-hand, and he pulled Emma around the corner, away from the light spilling out of the opening. In the dark, he bent his head and took her mouth with his, searing out any doubts she could have had. She was the one who missed a beat this time, but caught up quickly, winding her arms around his neck. The blanket dropped off her shoulders and she pressed herself impossibly closer. Sliding a hand into her hair, he tipped her head back, leaving her mouth to press his lips to the soft spot under her jaw, the silky skin at her throat and the hard curve of her collarbone.

Her hands moved down over his neck, her fingers fisting in the lapels of his vest and crushing his boutonniere. She repeated that soft noise she'd made in the arena the day before, and it shot hot shards of desire through his bloodstream. It sounded like surrender and wanting and he felt that to his core.

He could hear her heavy breaths; feel the goose bumps rising on her arms. Every damn thing about her was intoxicating in a way that was entirely different from the bottles he'd drowned himself in. He couldn't get close enough. That dress looked like heaven on, but with no zippers or buttons to speak of, he'd have to slide it over her head and expose her to the elements to get his hands on bare skin.

When he pulled back, her features were soft with wanting. Her lips were still parted, an open invitation to taste her again. He should have been inside raising another toast to his brother, but all he wanted was to take her upstairs to his bedroom and finish what he'd started. He groaned, dragging her against his chest for a beat. He took a minute to collect himself, sucking in a breath he hoped she didn't notice had hitched.

"People are going to start looking for us."

"Uh huh," she murmured.

"S'pose we should go back in?"

"Uh huh."

She finally lifted her head and he cupped her jaw, gently tracing his thumb across her lower lip.

"If that's what you mean by having tonight, I'd like to have every night," he teased, moving his fingers to slide over her hair, straightening what he'd mussed with his clumsy hands. "And then some."

SEVENTEEN

EMMA'S FATHER SPOTTED them the minute they stepped inside the tent and about ten seconds after they dropped their clasped hands between them. A slow song filtered over the speakers and just about everybody was dancing; even Kerri was spinning Gage around the floor. Emma caught a glimpse of her mother with Banks Montgomery and she knew what was coming.

"I'm gonna take this pretty little girl off your hands for a few minutes, Noah." Emma's father held his hand out for her and winked at her companion before pulling her toward the dance floor. While his technique was lacking, he made up for it in heart, and he rarely sat out a song once the floor was warmed up. Fast or slow, it didn't matter. She'd danced with her father hundreds of times. He would joke that he had two left feet but that didn't interfere with his love of the music. With one arm still in his brace, it made for an awkward posture, but he held her hand with his good arm and she held them together with a hand lightly on his shoulder.

"You having fun, sweetie?"

"It's a beautiful wedding. Completely what I imagined."

"Beautiful bride, too."

She nodded, and turned her head to see where Dane and Ren were dancing, barely moving. He held her close and she rested her head on his chest, completely wrapped up in one another as if nothing else mattered.

"I think they make each other really happy. And Dane deserves that," she concluded, turning back to her father.

"I know a few other people that deserve to be happy."

"Daddy..."

He shook his head, gave her a little spin, and then drew her in close again.

"Does being back home make you happy, Emma?"

She didn't reply quickly. Right now, still warm with the memory of Noah's hands in her hair, on her waist, his mouth on hers – right now, she could say she was happy in Three Rivers. But if she let herself think too much about it, it was hard to shake the memories of how she'd felt when she left, regardless of the apology that had made her ache. Had he really changed?

"I promise, I'm not going to try to guilt you into staying, and I don't know what Denver looked like for you, but seeing you spending time with Noah and Stephanie, riding Alamo...it *does* make me wonder what's so bad about Three Rivers," he continued.

She considered her father's words as she caught sight of Noah, who had taken her mother from Banks. She was laughing like a madwoman while Noah whirled her around the dance floor, a few beats too fast for the music that was playing. Her mother had always loved Noah, had probably never stopped, and if Emma was honest, she probably hadn't either. She put on a brave smile for her father.

"Nothing, actually. Nothing."

"Good. I know you have a contract to finish, but I'd like to see you around a little more often."

"I know, Daddy. You will."

In truth, coming home hadn't been as bad as she had anticipated. It was like when she was fourteen and she hadn't eaten dirt off the back of a horse in a few years. The longer the time stretched on since the last fall, the more she dreaded it. Until a bee sting had gotten her bucked off of Alamo in their first week together. Coming home to less pain and drama than she had expected was sort of like that fall when she'd realized she probably wouldn't die. Falling off had become quite a bit less intimidating after the first one. She could see herself coming home to Three Rivers for weekends and holidays, now. And just maybe, when the contract was over, she could see herself back here for good. And maybe not for Noah; maybe for herself.

"But more than anything, I'd like to see you happy. You deserve that. Wherever it is. Here or Denver. And whoever it's with—your team at Renegade, or..." He trailed off but his eyes tracked to Noah and she suppressed a groan. Her daddy was one of the most perceptive men she knew, so it didn't actually surprise her at all that he had figured out something might be going on. "Anyways. There's a lot more to life than satisfying your old dad. Do what makes *you* happy for as long as it does."

She pressed a kiss to her father's cheek right around the same time Noah and Myrna swung by them. With a knowing smile, Jonas smoothly reached out and extracted Myrna from Noah's arms while somehow managing to neatly deposit Emma into them.

He had a silly smirk on his face as he turned their bodies a couple of times, settling into the rhythm of the slow song considerably better than he had done with her mother. She could have almost sworn he'd paid her daddy off.

"So. Did he put in a good word for me?"

"Please tell me my father isn't your wingman."

He shrugged, brushing off the question and tugged her closer to his chest.

"Nah, but he's one of those people that stood by me when I needed a little extra confidence."

Emma raised a brow.

"Your father's a good man. Sometimes you just need a kind word when you're at your lowest. He gave that to me. More than once. *You* gave that to me. Also more than once."

"He's full of wisdom and knowledge, alright." She glanced over Noah's shoulder to where her father was spinning her mother around the dance floor, oblivious to her suspicious gaze. He was laughing jovially at something she'd said. He was happy. Even when Emma wasn't around, she suspected her parents had carved out a happy life here in Three Rivers. She watched them a moment, her heart full and her body warmed by the closeness of Noah's. This made her happy. She would do what made her happy for as long as it did.

EIGHTEEN

"I COULD REALLY go for pizza." Bent over, Noah frowned at the contents of Dane's fridge.

The party was still going on, but some of the older guests had headed home, including Emma's parents. He'd nearly done cartwheels when she'd walked to the property line with them and then told them not to wait up.

They hadn't even gone back to the tent. He'd snagged her hand and they'd used the cover of darkness to sneak into the big house. The only light was the one flooding from the open fridge, and in that wedge of illumination, he could see her bare, smooth legs. She kicked out of her ballet flats and slid up onto the counter beside the fridge. It was all he could do not to press his lips to the inside of her ankle and work his way up.

What little buzz he'd had was wearing off and a night of spinning around the dance floor had his stomach growling. He was starving but after that tempting kiss outside the tent, he wasn't sure which hunger to sate first.

"Too bad it's after midnight."

He straightened and looked at her. "And you didn't turn into a pumpkin. Imagine."

Letting the fridge door fall shut, he slipped into the v her legs made, running his fingers up her bare calves to rest on her knees.

"Aww," she teased, sliding her arms around his neck and pushing her fingers into his hair. "Are you disappointed?"

Tipping his head back, he caught her eyes and tentatively slid his fingers higher, under the fabric of her dress that draped over her thighs. A shiver of goose bumps lifted on her skin and she drew in a tight breath.

"You could never disappoint me."

He'd seen her at her best and her worst and everything in between. He knew he'd disappointed her—more than once—but he couldn't think of anything she could come up with that would put him off. She bent her head and brushed her lips over his lightly. She tasted just as sweet as the first time. *Forget the pizza.*

He pressed his fingers into her thighs and dragged her closer to the edge of the counter, closer to him, his intent clear. Just as their bodies drew together, her stomach let loose the loudest rumble he'd ever heard. She dropped her head back and laughed.

"Okay, okay, I get it." He reluctantly pulled himself away and jerked the fridge door open again, coming up with a handful of grapes, a chunk of cheddar cheese, a couple pieces of Ren's homemade jerky and a couple cans of beer.

"They're going to start a fire and have s'mores out there, you know." Emma said, sliding off the counter and back into her shoes as he assembled the food on a plate. Gage had informed everybody at least a half a dozen times during the party that there would be a fire and treats. It was probably the part of the wedding his nephew was the most excited about.

"I just got you all to myself; you think I want to share?" She stopped and raised a brow at him and he shook his head in response. "Not a chance. C'mere."

He reached out and tugged her to him again, pressing a kiss to her lips that was quick but searing.

"How much time have we actually gotten to spend alone together that didn't involve throwing hay for the horses or one of us intoxicated?"

She grinned and covered her face. "You're never going to let me live that down, are you?"

"Hey, this is the first time I've mentioned it." He lowered his voice, dropping his mouth close to her ear. "And only because I'd like to replay it a little differently."

What he said must have worked because she drew closer, tipped her head, and raked her teeth along his jaw lightly, not unlike the way she had in his bed. He groaned and slid an arm around her waist, leading her upstairs.

~

Emma lay on her back in Noah's big queen sized bed with her ankles crossed and her hands folded over her stomach. He'd gone downstairs to dispose of the plate and empty beer cans and she took the time alone as an opportunity to look around the room he'd called his since childhood. Of course, they'd spent much of their time together on horseback, in the barn, and in the company of others but she'd been in here lots of times. Just...never in this context.

She heard Noah coming back up the stairs and a burst of butterflies shot out of her belly and through her bloodstream. He slipped in the door and smiled at her like he was relieved to find her still there. Crossing the floor, he unbuttoned the cuffs of his dress shirt. He'd long ago gotten rid of the vest. All of a sudden, she was nervous.

"What are you doing?"

"Getting comfortable." He laughed, nodding to her reclined position. "Just like you did."

And with that, he climbed into the bed, stretching out beside her in a motion that was all too smooth to be unnerving. It was another of those things they'd done time and time again in the most casual of contexts, but this was something entirely different considering the circumstances.

She turned her head to look at him, her eyes tracing the planes of his face. His strong jaw, the stubble, those unruly curls, all of them so familiar to her; they'd always belonged to the boy she called a friend, but tonight they belonged to a man she wanted. He shifted up on his elbow, watching her, and she let her fingers follow the trail of her eyes. When she passed her palm over his jaw, he turned his face into it with his eyes closed, and reached up to cover her hand with his, letting out a slow breath.

"I'm not going to do anything you're not comfortable with, Em, but damnit if I don't wanna make love to you tonight. That dress..." He opened his eyes and liberally let them roam over her body, like he wanted her to see the hunger in his eyes, the way they consumed every part of her body. His words and the rawness of his gaze were a hot shot of desire to her bloodstream, leaving her breathless. Nobody had ever looked at her or spoken to her quite this way.

"What about this dress?" She slipped her hand out from under his and smoothed her lacy dress. She'd bought it in Denver but never worn it; her homesickness manifested in shopping from time to time. Usually, she regretted it. Tonight, the look in his eyes erased any trace of buyer's remorse she'd had about the dress.

He wet his lips, his eyes darting to where her hand had come to rest on her hip.

"I think it looks incredible on you, but I'd be interested to see how it looks on the floor."

Despite her nerves, the dark undercurrent of his tone made her want to sit up and slip it right off over her head without a second thought. Instead, he shifted his hand to where hers rested and slid his fingers under hers, tightening them against her hip and tilting her body toward his to meet her lips for a kiss that made her dizzy.

Emma sucked in her stomach and a breath as his hand moved up her hip, under her skirt. When he hit the fabric of those underwear she'd wrangled herself into, he paused, lifted his mouth from her throat and raised an eyebrow at her.

"What the hell is that?"

"Spanx." She blushed. "They hold you in, make a nicer body shape."

He tipped his head down, his fingers creeping to the waistband and sliding underneath. She shivered as his touch tickled her sensitive skin. "Is that so?"

She swallowed and nodded.

"Let me tell you something about your 'body shape', Em." He pressed his lips to her jaw. "It needs no improvement. You're a beautiful woman. In a t-shirt and jeans, or this amazing dress."

She let out the breath she was holding when he used his fingers to slide the shapewear down her hips.

Her body was begging for more of his touch but her brain flushed her cheeks with an embarrassing blush. She squeezed her eyes shut. She wanted this, all of it. But she didn't want him to see her body, despite his words. It was okay if Emma-as-a-friend had thirty or forty extra pounds, but Emma-as-a-lover should have been immaculate—like the other women she'd seen him date.

"Hey." He slowed his hand sliding across her stomach, over the fabric of her dress again. "What's wrong? If you're not comfortable with this, I'll stop. You know I will, Em."

She opened her eyes. How could she articulate this? It hadn't been like this with anyone else, because no one else mattered. But Noah – he mattered, much as she tried to tell herself different. If the kiss had been a line they couldn't uncross, this was a transatlantic flight where they burned their plane at the end and could never go back.

"I don't want you to stop."

He shook his head, sliding his hand a little higher, to her ribcage. He tightened his fingers for a second to give her a reassuring squeeze.

"Then?"

She let out a long breath and closed her eyes.

"Maybe we could turn out the lights?"

She cracked one eye open when she felt his hand move from her stomach and saw him reach over to turn off the lamp on the bedside table. The moon was big and bright and there was still light from the tent streaming in the window, but it was mostly shadows. It wasn't the pitch dark she would have preferred, but it would do. He turned back to her, leaned over her and cradled her jaw in his palm, forcing her eyes to his.

"Is this okay?"

"Yes." She breathed a sigh of relief and reached up to rub her fingers across the stubble on his jaw, tugging on a strand of hair that curled behind his ear. She couldn't see his eyes, but it was more comfortable this way.

He kissed her soundly, dropped his hand down, and slid it across her belly to her opposite hip. Bunching the fabric of her dress in his fingers, he found bare flesh again and traced over the sensitive skin at the top of her thigh. Her insides quaked. His lips made a line across her jaw and found her throat.

"I want to make you feel amazing, Emma. But anything that doesn't feel right, tell me. We've always been able to talk. This is no different."

She nodded but she was preoccupied by the trek his fingers made toward the apex of her thighs, and the way he drew in on her pulse when he found it. Her whole body tensed when his fingers reached their destination and then relaxed when he slid his thumb along the very center of her. Her head dropped back and a soft noise slipped past her lips. She felt his mouth twist into a smile against her skin, and he nicked his teeth across her neck as he nudged her again, sending sparks of pleasure shooting through her bloodstream. She tucked herself closer to him, wanting his touch more than anything she'd ever remembered wanting.

"Okay?" His breath rasped out of him, but he tipped his head back to catch her eyes and she nodded, her breathing as harsh as his. He was turned on, and that aroused her more than she already was. Shifting her hips up, she willed his fingers just a bit lower. Like he'd read her mind, he slid a finger down, pressing up with the pad of his thumb at the same time. A soft cry bubbled out of her throat before she could think about it.

With his face pressed into her neck, he moved slowly, deliberately, and her body arched into his decadent touch. Being with Noah had always made her feel good but this was another dimension of goodness she hadn't known existed. Letting out a low moan, she felt herself rising to the crest of that feeling and heard his breath hitch next to her just a second before she lost herself completely.

NINETEEN

NOAH ROLLED ONTO his back and eased Emma against his chest while she struggled to catch her breath. The sound of her calling out his name still rang in his ears. She was exquisite, incredible, but he had expected no less. This was Emma, his Emma. He pressed a kiss to her damp temple and gave her a squeeze.

Her dress was tangled high on her waist and he shifted, helping her lift it off over her head, pleased that she didn't resist. By now, his eyes had adjusted to the dark and he took in the sight of her—smooth, soft curves of delicate whiteness where she wasn't tanned from the Colorado summer; heavy breasts and a rounded stomach. All of it appealing, all of it desirable. All of it made him hard as hell. She had no idea.

It had been a surprise when she'd been nervous; he'd wanted her with a sureness he'd never possessed before, but the satisfied purr she made when he moved again and began to trace his mouth along the curves he hadn't yet seen told him he'd communicated at least a little bit of his desire to her.

He drew his head back, let out a breath, and shook his head. With her hand tangled in his hair, her fingernails against his scalp, she smiled quizzically.

"What?"

"I can't believe I'm this lucky." He lowered his head and pressed his lips just above her navel, never breaking eye contact. Something passed over her eyes and he knew he'd crossed into uncomfortable territory for her. He resolved that he would change that; prove to her just how delectable he found her body to be. If it meant worshiping her this way every day for the rest of their lives, well that was exactly what he would do, and happily.

She let out a sigh as he traced a line with his tongue from her navel to the delicious valley between her full breasts.

"I mean it. There isn't a thing about you that doesn't drive me crazy, Em."

She didn't reply, but she didn't try to brush off his compliment, either. Moving a bit higher, he peppered kisses over her collarbone until he heard her draw a deep breath and she took her fingers out of his hair and tugged at the buttons at the throat of his shirt.

"Let's make this fair," she murmured, and he pulled back to let her help him unbutton the shirt. He shouldered it off and held his breath as she moved her fingers now to the fly of his jeans. Her wanting him was almost as hot as the sounds she'd made as she came; as *he'd* made her come. The thought, combined with her trembling fingers sliding his zipper down made him let out that breath he'd been holding, and when they slipped into his boxers to touch him, he nearly came apart.

He shifted up her body and took her mouth in an attempt to hide the fact that he felt like a teenaged boy rounding third base for the first time, but he couldn't suppress a groan at her light touch. It bolstered her confidence, because she slid her hands over his abdomen and hooked her fingers into the waistband of his jeans and boxers, tugging them downward. He shifted his hips to help, and then moved away for the briefest of moments to drag them down over his knees and kick them off before repositioning himself over her.

"Fair now?" He teased, his mouth close to her ear. He loved the friction of her skin against his, her body so wondrously soft and receptive. He scraped his stubble lightly along her jaw and she squirmed, laughing as she put a hand on his hip and then slid it up his spine to rest between his shoulder blades.

"Close," she murmured, pressing him closer to her.

~

They were so near, Emma was thankful for the cover of darkness to hide the flush creeping up her neck. She wanted this, badly, and he clearly did, too, but that didn't stop her feelings of inadequacy and awkwardness. They'd seen one another in every conceivable state—good, bad and otherwise. Nothing should have embarrassed either one of them. But to hear him say that he was lucky to have access to her body, to bring her to what she was pretty sure was the best orgasm she'd ever had with just a few flicks of his fingers, to hear his sounds of appreciation when she timidly touched him in the few ways she'd never touched him before—it was overwhelming and unnerving and exciting, all at once.

She struggled to catch a breath as he brushed a bit of hair away from her face and pressed a kiss to the end of her nose, the most chaste of touches made erotic by their positions. He'd moved to a spot in the space between her legs and was somehow holding himself a fraction of an inch away from her, but she could feel the heat from his body and the muscles in his back shifting as he supported himself.

Drawing a hand from thigh to knee, created a space for him to get closer still, and with a tight breath, he eased into her, snugging his body up to the v he'd made.

She pressed her lips together and held her breath, her fingers tightening into the muscles of his back. They strained under her fingers and she took a moment to savor, to ground herself. Panic passed over his features, and she slid her hand from his shoulders into his hair, drawing his head down to meet his mouth. When she pulled away, her lips hovered a hair's breadth away from his and she let out a shuddering breath. They were on the cusp of something much greater than these weeks together; something larger than their years before that. She smiled, curling her fingertips against his scalp.

"Don't stop."

He tipped his hips against hers, bringing them closer together, shifted back, then tipped them again. A rush of sensation, both emotional and physical threatened to swallow her up as her head dropped back against the pillow. She felt his fingertips tracing along her hairline and opened her eyes to find a relieved smile playing over his lips.

They found a rhythm together that felt as comfortable and intimate as their friendship was, as if they'd always been lovers, as if their bodies were meant to fit together in just this way. And too soon, Emma felt her body rising toward a second orgasm. Biting down on her lower lip, she held Noah to her, tight, desperate to hold this for just a bit longer.

It was a perfect moment, one in which she didn't have to think about Denver, or the implications of sneaking away from his brother's wedding to do this, or what the rumor mill might say when they got hold of it. She could focus on the incredible way his steady, confident movements stoked the fire of her desire, the way his familiar face, lax with the pleasure of touching her and making love to her, drowned out everything else.

He breathed her name like a prayer and a second later, he followed her as she came apart.

TWENTY

NOAH CLIMBED OUT of his truck and let the door fall shut behind him. He didn't bother to lock it—none of the locals ever did. Same went for houses, but he'd locked his up after that night he'd brought Emma there from the bar. He hadn't been back since. It made more sense to stick close to the ranch; that's where Emma was, so that's where he wanted to be, even with Dane and Ren gone off for their honeymoon and Kerri and Gage staying with his parents.

He nodded in greeting to Banks, who was coming out of Sawyer's with a bag of groceries.

"Afternoon, Noah."

"Banks. Groceries for Nan?" He gestured to the bags.

Aida Montgomery was technically only Banks' grandmother but Noah couldn't think of a kid in Three Rivers who didn't call her 'Nan'. A retired schoolteacher who was still active in the community, she'd raised Banks and his brother, Nate, and as a result, Banks had never ventured far from Three Rivers or Nan. The pair had an exceptionally close relationship, and while he didn't live in her basement anymore, he still visited her every day despite her protests, brought her groceries, and ran errands for her.

"Sure are. She's been out at the high school all day doing something or other. I knew she wouldn't have time."

"Tell her I said hello." Noah had almost as many warm memories of Nan as Banks likely did.

"Will do." Banks turned to go to his cruiser. "Say, you ought to bring Emma by to visit. She'd love to see the pair of you."

"We'll swing by," Noah promised, and pushed open the door to Sawyer's.

The grocery store hadn't changed, not since he was a young boy, from the butcher counter to the candy lining the single checkout at the front. He picked up a basket and passed through the aisles of the store, locating the things he needed with little difficulty. He hardly slowed until he got to that single checkout and saw who was scanning groceries three customers ahead. His heart sunk straight to the bottom of his belly and he considered abandoning the basket and going elsewhere, but that would require a twenty five minute drive each direction. Sawyer's was the one option in town.

Clenching his jaw, he waited in line, feeling lower and lower the closer he got to the register.

There was no way he could walk out of his store feeling like anything but a bum.

"Noah." Layla Sullivan didn't sound any happier to see him than he felt, though he'd apologized a thousand times over. When he'd sobered up, he'd taken a loan from his parents to pay off her hospital bill, and apart from his mortgage, every penny since had gone to them. He was still paying it off, and he didn't hold it against her. He was the one who had made the mistakes, here. She kept promising it was okay, but learned by now that 'okay' didn't ease the awkwardness. Either way, he didn't know what else he could do to make up for the way he'd derailed her life.

"Hey Layla. How are you?"

She looked as uncomfortable answering as he felt asking, but finally responded. "I'm okay, thanks."

"I thought you were working over at Dr. Fields' office?" That was the safest place she could be. He went into Sawyer's a hell of a lot more than the town doctor's office. He only knew she was working there because of Finn, who had had a relatively close relationship with Dr. Fields' staff because of Sunny's cancer.

"Oh. Four days a week. When they're closed, I pick up shifts here." She shrugged, swiping his items across the bar code reader and deftly punching in numbers on things that wouldn't scan. She was clearly here more than a couple of hours a week.

It was barely believable that there could be

wrong side of the tracks in a place as small as Three Rivers, but if it existed, that's where the Sullivans lived. Daddy and mama both out of work and a whole passel of kids, ranging in age from Kyle, at Kerri's age, to Jimmy, who had graduated with Dane.

Layla was a sweetheart, which was more than he could say for Jimmy or any of the other boys—but she had been in the wrong place at the wrong time. He hadn't meant to hurt her, but then he hadn't meant to hurt *anyone*.

"Gotcha," he said, digging into his pocket.

"$22.05. You making dinner for Ren and Dane?" She gestured to the items he'd purchased. All the fixings for a big steak dinner, minus the steak of course—Baylor beef stocked the freezer at home. He handed over two bills and she put the change on the counter in front of him instead of into his hand.

"Oh, uh...no, they're actually gone on their honeymoon. Just...dinner for myself." He collected the coins and singles off the countertop. She would find out sooner or later about him and Emma, but for now, telling her would be a bit like pouring salt on a wound.

"Oh, well...have a good night." She handed him his receipt and he picked up the paper bag and headed for the door.

Once in his truck, he dialed Emma's cell phone. After a few rings she picked up, and he felt relief wash away the discomfort.

"Hey, you had dinner yet?"

"Mmm...no. Mama's just got some meatloaf in the oven."

"You wanna see what I learned?" He smiled, shifted into reverse, and then drive, cradling the phone between his cheek and shoulder. Just the sound of her voice soothed him, but the prospect of seeing her put the uncomfortable conversation he'd just had out of his mind altogether.

"Hang on," she said, and then he heard her speaking to her parents. "I'm gonna go eat with Noah tonight. He's lonesome up there in the big house."

"Hey, come on!" He protested. She laughed over the receiver and he smiled. "But that means yes, right?"

"Yes, I wanna see what you learned."

"I'm just in town, be home in ten."

As he steered the truck back toward the Baylor ranch and thought of Emma there waiting for him, he couldn't help but envision a life where she was *always* at home, waiting for him. Their home, a little slice of land carved out somewhere nearby. A half a dozen barrel horses in training, and a cozy log cabin with an open hearth to snuggle up in front of when the winter winds got desperate. A dog and a little nursery for a towheaded baby boy who'd have blue eyes just like his mama.

~

Emma sat on the steps of the big Baylor

house waiting for Noah's truck to roll in the drive. Rex curled into a ball at her feet, happy as long as her fingers aimlessly scratched his ruff between his shoulder blades. She felt silly as a little thrill of anticipation went through her when she heard his truck's motor. Rex perked but was happy to stay parked as long as her fingers were buried in his fur.

Two weeks ago, she wouldn't have bet her life on things arranging this way. But now, she knew what it felt like to be the focus of Noah Baylor's attentions and her world felt like a whole different place. If their friendship had been goodness, whatever *this* was was perfection. They snuck long looks and little kisses in the barn, when her parents could walk in on them any time, stoking the fire for when they could come together in the empty Baylor house. She made herself blissfully ignorant of the fact that the newlyweds would be home soon and that her father's appointments at Dr. Fields' office were becoming progressively more positive.

They would cross that bridge when they got there, but for now, she was following her father's advice.

A silly grin spread across her face when she saw his truck pull in. He waved, shifted into park and climbed out of the truck with a brown paper bag from Sawyer's. Finally, she got to her feet.

"Hey," she said, and not for the first time, she felt a little bit shy when they came back together in private after an absence. Here he was, as someone entirely different to her than goodfriend, inside-joke Noah. He was all of that and more; Noah with a gentle loving touch and an intuition about her body that she didn't even have.

He set the bag on the hood of the truck and pulled her to him. She expected a kiss in greeting, but his lips pressed to her jaw and moved to the soft spot behind her ear. His teeth tugged at the lobe of her ear and a shiver slid over her skin, thinking of the other things he did with those teeth and that mouth. Even despite his protests, it still felt strange to know that Noah Baylor wanted her this way. *Had* wanted her this way, even before she'd become 'the girl from away'. He pressed his stubbled cheek against hers and drew in a long breath.

"You're silly. You just saw me not four hours ago."

"I know." She felt his cheek swell as he smiled, then finally pulled back. "That's too long."

"What will you do when I'm back in Denver? That's a two hour drive each way—you'll just get home and won't have time to get back to the city before you're crazy missing me again," she teased.

They really hadn't addressed her return to Denver though they knew it would come eventually, and a part of her wondered if, now that they had established that they wanted one another just about as badly as she wanted her job in Denver, maybe more, he would try to keep her here again.

She still received texts almost daily from Allison, looking for advice on rehab for their new arrival, Encore. The horse and his rider had been hit by a car and by Emma's estimation, fixing his physical problems were the least of the challenges facing him. She wanted to see his case through to the end; it motivated her almost as much as the legalities of the contract she'd signed.

And on top of all of that, she had to prove to herself that she could do it. Walk away from Noah, stand on her own two feet and *want* him more than she needed him. She wanted to know that she didn't want him just because he felt like home and that he didn't want her just because she was there.

She tightened her arms around his neck and held him to her for just a second longer. Home felt pretty damn good. Finally, she released him and pulled back.

"Okay, time to show me what you got."

Forty minutes later, Emma sat at the big table in the Baylor kitchen and watched Noah shuffle around, putting the finishing touches on a butter-basted steak, potatoes and vegetables. He looked mostly comfortable, but still hesitated from time to time and looked like he was reciting instructions to himself. She'd offered to help, but he insisted she should sit at the table with a beer and relax, so she'd obliged. She still found herself wanting to steady his hand or show him a more efficient method, but she'd drown it out with a swig of beer and was on her second can, now.

She narrowed her eyes as he laid plates out and took care to arrange the food like something she'd see on a restaurant plate in Denver.

"So, Noah's strangely culinary talented twin brother...when does the *real* Noah show up? The last time I saw you, you were doing well to heat a can of beans." She'd cooked for him dozens of times because it was better than seeing him eat something that was unfailingly either burnt to a crisp or raw.

"Well," he said, wiping his hands on a dish towel hanging from the front of the oven. "Although I am an extraordinarily talented rodeo cowboy, I can't afford a personal chef *and* a mortgage. So, out of necessity..." He set the food onto the table with a flourish.

Emma eyed the plates, her brows raised as she poked the steak, which looked damn near perfect, with her fork.

"Come on, I wouldn't poison you...on purpose," he teased, taking the seat across from her. "You'll be impressed, I promise."

She kept up her suspicious shtick as she cut into the steak, selecting a small piece and putting it in her mouth. Chewing carefully, she tipped her head. He watched her with an earnest expression. She could tell he was eager to impress her. Finally she swallowed, and shook her head.

"Damn."

"Damn?"

"Well, it might be the fact that it's homegrown beef..." She loved her mama's cooking but this steak would beat Myrna's meatloaf any day of the week. "But it's pretty good."

A handsome and slightly relieved smile

crossed his features. He looked particularly proud of himself as he cut into his own steak.

"So who taught you?" she asked.

He shrugged innocently.

"I know you didn't learn yourself. Out with it." She waved her steak knife in his direction.

"Steph."

"When?"

"Yesterday. I just lucked out that it turned out this good. And also...Baylor beef. That's a big help."

She shook her head and sliced another section off the meat. They ate in silence for a while; the food was so good she couldn't even rib him too much for just learning yesterday. As he finished his plate, she slid hers away and pushed back from the table.

"So what's for dessert?"

The look he gave her near dissolved her into a puddle right there.

"There's this little matter of Cutter Anderson's annual end-of-summer bonfire before any dessert can be had."

She made a face. Dane and Ren would come home soon and this little game of house they played would come to an end. She wanted to draw every ounce of pleasure and happiness out of this time, in private, because the second Finn or Dane got a whiff of this, there'd be no end to the tormenting she'd get.

"Didn't he stop doing those in high school?"

"No, we just stopped going." Noah laughed. "Fall rodeo weekend started happening about the same time and we were too busy chasing barrels, remember?"

"And remind me why we're going to start going again?"

Noah rose from the table, taking her plate. He dropped a scrap of meat to Rex, who had been snoozing under the table but got up anxiously when chairs started scraping across the floor.

"Because it's fun. And Steph made me promise to bring you to prove I hadn't accidentally poisoned you." He teased, pulling her out of her chair and into his arms. Any opportunity he had, he brought her closer, and she couldn't say she minded. She looped her arms around his neck as he continued. "Come on, no more complaining. If you don't have fun, you can drive my truck for a week."

"If I recall correctly, the last time you wagered your truck, you stacked the odds in your favor."

"I cannot tell a lie. I fully intend to do that again." He grinned, pressed a kiss to her lips, and herded her toward the door with a playful swat to her backside.

TWENTY-ONE

NOAH PASSED A glance at Emma as they pulled into the field beside the Anderson ranch. The family had been struggling with crop returns the last couple of seasons but Cutter seemed unaffected by the troubles his family was experiencing; his party was in full swing. Noah would have passed judgment that Cutter had never really grown up except it would have been hypocritical.

She looked like she took a steeling breath and he smiled. His intent was twofold, here. He *had* promised Stephanie he'd produce a live, unpoisoned Emma at the party, but he also wanted to take her out and show her off.

He put the truck in park and reached over to squeeze her hand. "We'll stop in and say hello and if it's not for you, then we'll go home."

She raised a brow at him. "And what would we do at home?"

He shrugged innocently.

She slipped out of the truck and he followed suit, falling into stride beside her and reaching down to grab her hand again as they headed toward the fire pit.

A circle of pickups were backed up near the fire and every tail gate was down and covered in bodies. It looked like a scene from a country music video and he heard Emma let out a breath. She smoothed her free hand over her long jeans. He knew this had never been her preferred scene but there was little to do in Three Rivers besides Danny's and the dance hall. She'd never had much in common with the girls in town; they all wanted to date ropers and racers and Emma had always wanted to *be* one. There *were* more bare legs and Daisy Dukes than he could shake a stick at, but he barely saw them, his mind fixated on the girl next to him.

He caught sight of Stephanie and Jamie curled into one another on the back of his quarter ton and when she saw Emma, she waved frantically. A six pack sat on the tailgate beside them and they looked as in love as they had in high school. Noah guided her across the middle of the circle of trucks toward her friend with a chuckle at Steph's exaggerated antics.

"You're not poisoned!" Stephanie laughed, opening her arms for Emma and squeezing her tight. Over Emma's shoulder, she gave Noah a big thumbs up.

"No, it was actually pretty good." Emma admitted with a grin while Jamie reached around his wife and pushed a bottle of beer toward her. She took it and cracked the top off, taking a long pull as she settled in beside her friends. "I can't believe you taught him that."

Steph blew on her knuckles, and polished them on her shoulders, then shrugged. "He showed up with a bag full of groceries and a desperate look in his eye. I would have shut the door in his face, but he said it was for you...and after our coffee date, I couldn't resist helping."

Noah watched Emma roll her eyes when Stephanie gave her a big, exaggerated wink. He could only imagine what they'd discussed during the coffee date. Then Steph turned to him.

"And *you* owe me a case of beer."

"Ah, right. It's in the truck, hang on." Feeling brazen, he stepped forward and pressed a kiss to Emma's forehead. She blushed, but she smiled, too, and he counted it as a win.

He hurried back to the truck, retrieving the case of light beer from the bed, then turned back toward the party, only to find himself face to face with Layla once again.

Her eyes darted to the side; looking for a quick escape, he guessed. And he couldn't blame her.

"Fancy seeing you twice in one day." She pasted a smile onto her face that he could tell was forced. "How did your dinner go?"

A quick scan of the guests at the party had produced her brother, Jimmy, halfway around the fire from the Turner's truck, but he hadn't seen her.

And now he felt lower than low. It had been a roller coaster of a day.

"It was good." With his free hand, he rubbed the back of his neck, glanced back toward the party, and then back to Layla. "Are you heading out already?"

"I've got to work in the morning. Dr. Fields' office." She smiled, shrugged a little. "You have a good time with Emma."

It would have been easier if she had been angrier, if she didn't try to be as polite and friendly as she had been before he'd spotted her across the bar at Danny's. But he didn't sense an ounce of animosity in her voice. As with every hand that had been dealt to her in life thus far, she politely accepted it.

"Layla, look... I..."

"You don't have to say anything, Noah." She shook her head, a sad smile lifting one corner of her lips.

But he did. He'd brought Emma here, and he was sure she'd seen. In a town as small as Three Rivers, the odds of running into her were high, and he couldn't hide his life from Layla forever out of pity.

"I do, Layla. Or else we're going to play this awkward back and forth game for the rest of our lives."

She looked confused, and a little hurt, and he wished they had something more in common than the baby that hadn't been. Truth was, as nice a girl as Layla was, once the whiskey was gone, so was whatever had drawn them together in the first place. He sensed that this was about more than just their failure to launch as anything more than friends with benefits, but it wasn't his place.

"I hurt you and used you to try to fix the hurt in *me*. And it wasn't right. Or fair."

She pursed her lips, dropped her eyes, and then drew in a breath and looked back up at him. "I knew you didn't want *me*, Noah."

"That's not true..." He knew it was a placating lie even as it came out of his mouth.

"It's a small town and the pool of candidates runs out quick. I know you wanted Emma. I'd have to be blind not to. And nobody would expect anything different. I just wanted that baby." She wrapped her arms around her mid section and Noah ached. No amount of apologies or paid-off hospital bills could give her what she wanted. He could never be responsible for the happy ending she needed. "It's pretty sad, but that was the best thing that had happened to me. Anyway. You can't help who you love or don't love."

"Someday, somebody is going to come along and love you the way you deserve, Layla. Completely, and unfailingly. And they'll give you a *family*, not just a lonely pregnancy." He truly believed it. She was a nice girl, with a kind heart.

"I know," she said, and the smile that had looked so sad looked more peaceful now.

"Can you ever forgive me for the way I mistreated you, Layla?"

"A year ago? No. Today?" She shrugged,

shifted one foot to the other. "Time, and nothing else, heals a lot of things. I forgive you. I deserve to be happy, and I know you can't give that to me; not because you don't want to. You just *can't*, and that's okay; I don't want you to. Goodnight, Noah."

"Goodnight, Layla."

She gave him one more smile, stronger this time. He watched her walk away, floored by her capacity for mercy when he didn't deserve it. She was a smarter, more resilient woman than he'd ever given her credit for. He'd underestimated her at so many turns.

He let that soak in for a moment before returning to the party.

TWENTY-TWO

"WELL, HE DID a good job, so you must be an excellent teacher." Emma squeezed her friend's shoulders and sought Noah out in the bodies milling around the fire with acoustic guitars and bottles of beer. Cutter had called out to him just before he'd started across the grass toward him. She found him just a beat before a petite blonde with a slim waist and a mile and a half of leg showing slid her hand down his arm.

Emma didn't recognize her, but the girl seemed *way* too familiar with Noah to be a stranger. He turned, seemed surprised to see the girl, but not unhappy, and gave her a stiff hug when she held her arms out. Emma slid her eyes back to Stephanie, pretending to be interested as she talked her way through all of Noah's blunders while she'd shown him how to sear the steak. With her face burning, and cursing herself for caring, Emma watched them in her peripheral vision.

She swallowed hard and tried to focus on Stephanie's words. They were talking, now. Noah cast a glance in the direction of the truck. In the quiet of his bedroom, tucked inside the door of the feed stall, when he put his hands on her, she could forget that she wasn't the type of girl that he normally dated. But here it was, plain as day.

Her friend saw her glance toward the fire again and followed her eyes. She looped her arm around Emma's waist and tugged her into her side.

"Oh hun, don't worry. He never learned to cook for *her*."

It wasn't what Emma needed to hear. Not even close. There were women she knew about because she'd witnessed it, but there was a whole two year period that was dark. Had he had an actual girlfriend? How many women had stayed over at that house in town? And how many of them looked like this, the polar opposite of her?

She stiffened as he stepped out of the conversation and headed back toward them. The entire time he strode across the yard, she told herself not to be this girl. The jealous one. The one who thinks, despite her partner's insistence, that she's never good enough. The one in need of constant reassurance because every day the media shows her that her body won't measure up. It was futile. She'd known Noah, and his preferences, too long to be able to put it away.

~

Noah dragged himself away from...what was her name, Cindy? She'd surprised the hell out of him, sneaking up behind him like that while he was still reeling from his conversation with Layla. Another stupid mistake. He barely remembered the night at Danny's that had brought her into his bed, but she remembered it, too well, apparently. He'd been a drunken, shitty mess, and he hadn't been particularly kind to her, either. He couldn't figure out why she had even bothered to say hello to him now, never mind inviting him to step away from the party for a few minutes.

His steps faltered as he approached the Turners' truck. *Something happened.* How in the hell could something happen in the fifteen minutes since he'd left her side? All he knew for sure was that Emma's face had changed, and she was snugged in as close to Stephanie as she should have been to him. The three of them squished together on the tailgate almost looked like Jamie had a second wife and there wasn't a spot for him.

Oblivious to whatever tension was knitting amongst the girls, Jamie held out a bottle of beer and Noah settled near him, leaning against the box of the truck. Truthfully, he didn't have much in common with Jamie but it was better than the vacant expression in Emma's eyes right now. She emptied the bottle she was holding and slid off the tailgate, headed for the huge galvanized tub of ice and beer that was set up near the house. He thought to follow her but held back.

"Okay, Steph. What's going on?" He asked

when Emma was safely out of earshot, taking the spot she'd been sitting in.

"How much does she know about when she's been gone?"

Stephanie had definitely seen some of Noah's shittiest moments—most of the town had—so she knew there had been more than a few indiscretions.

"She doesn't really want to talk about it."

He wanted to curse, but instead, he lifted the bottle to his lips, telling himself this was the only drink tonight. Maybe it had been a mistake to bring her here, but if they were to have any kind of future, they were going to run into women he'd spent time with while she'd been gone. It was a small town, and the list, especially in the six months following her departure, was long.

There was a lot of ground he still had to cover with Emma, but now he had something to protect, and he had to tread carefully.

"I think you're going to have to talk about it now."

TWENTY-THREE

"HEEEEY EMMA." CUTTER raised his bottle to Emma when she got to his makeshift bar.

She'd rarely seen the bartender so much as tipsy. Apparently, his parties were an opportunity to let loose. She dug through the ice and pulled up a beer that she wished was a bottle of whiskey. Wiping the label off, she straightened.

"Glad to see you two here tonight," Cutter said.

She nodded, but she didn't feel much like talking. She was acutely aware of the location of that little slip of a blonde at eight o'clock, and she hated that she'd kept tabs on her once Noah had walked away from her.

"I figured after the wedding, we'd see you two out and about a bit more often." Cutter winked, teasing.

She was a fool to think that nobody had picked up on what was happening at Dane and

Ren's wedding, but she'd convinced herself that everyone was so busy focusing on the newlyweds that they didn't have time to notice. Cutter saw everything, it was his job.

"Oh, we aren't..." She didn't know why she bothered to try to deny, and faded off, gesturing with her free hand.

"Like hell you aren't." Cutter snorted. His personality could be a little prickly but Emma knew he meant no harm. "Well, maybe *you* aren't, but he sure is."

Cutter nodded past her to where Noah was sitting on the tailgate, his eyes locked on her. She pursed her lips. Suddenly, she felt silly. Clearly, he had his options, and the option he'd picked was *her*. She could feel it, hotter than the changed air above the fire he watched her through.

"Yeah," she breathed. She raised her bottle to dismiss herself from her conversation with Cutter and turned to find Stephanie and Jamie gone and Noah all alone.

"C'mere," he murmured when she got to him, spreading his legs to make a space for her. He set his bottle aside and put an arm around her waist, settling her against one of his thighs.

"What are you doing?" Suspicion melted out when she felt the warmth of his body curled around hers. *He's picking me.* The realization warmed her as much as his body did.

A funny smile crossed his features and he shrugged, pressing a kiss to her jaw.

"Cutter was talking to you for too long."

She couldn't resist laughing at that. Cutter was far from her type. A good friend to have, and that was absolutely all.

"Trust me, Cutter is *not* a threat."

"Everybody's a threat." He laughed, but it cut too close to the bone for her.

"Who was that girl?" She hated the words even as they came out of her mouth. She tried to keep her tone casual, but the undercurrent of jealousy was plain as day, and she hated that, too.

He gave her a long look, like he was considering his words. When he spoke again, he was careful.

"Cindy Warden. Sondra's cousin. She showed up a couple of months after you left."

She nodded, looked into the crowd and spotted the girl trying her luck with Jimmy Sullivan.

"Don't worry about her, Em." He gave her a squeeze when she didn't respond. "I told her I was here with my girlfriend." *Girlfriend.* The word felt too tight and not tight enough all at once.

"What if you hadn't been here with me?" *Stop. Stop. Do not pass go.*

"Why are we going down this road, Em? I *am* here with you." Noah's brow furrowed. "Yes, I slept with her. Once. You shut me down every time I tried to talk about this, remember?"

His voice was tight; she could tell he didn't want to talk about this right here, right now, but he *had* tried to talk about it before. This was her own fault. She had been okay with hearing the apologies but really not what the apologies had been *for*.

"I just..." She searched for the words but they were hard coming. "I know she's your type, and I'm not..." As she spoke, Noah's brow drew tighter. She wanted to back out of the conversation in a hurry but she'd already come too far; the damage was done. In her mind, it seemed perfectly rational, but saying the words out loud made her feel silly.

"You're not what?" His eyes were hard and he hadn't loosened his grip on her. "Say it, Em."

"Where did Steph and Jamie go?"

He frowned, tipping her hips so she was facing him, jerking her body tight to his. It took her by surprise, and matched the intensity in his face.

"Just say it, Em, so I can tell you you're wrong."

She clenched her jaw, letting out a quick breath through her nose.

"I'm not your type." She couldn't meet his eyes when she said the words.

"You don't think so?"

She nodded, feeling tears rising in her throat. How did she get here? From angry, to in love, to self-deprecating. It wasn't her at all. He did funny things to her, like scaring her away from Three Rivers for two whole years. And the stronger the strange emotions, the worse she felt, a cycle of guilt that made her head spin, and she couldn't get off the carousel no matter how hard she tried.

"You're wrong," he said, simply. His next words were low, just for her. "You're wrong, because ever since Dane's wedding, I can't stop thinking about your soft body stretched out on my bed, your hair spilled over my pillow, the deliciously soft parts that fit against my body perfectly, and the way you fit into those jeans. Because the best parts of my day are those little kisses we sneak in the barn. And because I can't think of a better thing in the world than loving someone who knows me, right down to my soul."

Her heart jack-hammered in her throat at his words, her body paralyzed with...what was that? Fear?

"If you need me to stand up on this tailgate and shout it to the stars, I'll do it."

That jump-started her again. She put her hand on his shoulder, laughing nervously. There was no doubt in her mind that he would make true on the threat if she didn't put a stop to it right away.

"That's completely unnecessary."

"I will." He stood up, slipping his hands under the hem of her shirt and she felt his fingers press into what she'd always considered unattractive love handles. Despite what her brain had been trying to tell her, her body heated at his touch. "I don't care who sees or what they say. You're it for me, Emma. Always have been."

It was getting deep and uncomfortable, and Emma shifted. Where the hell had Steph and Jamie gone? She looked over his shoulder, into the dark, hoping to find their shapes, but she knew they'd probably taken tonight's child-free opportunity to go *be* those horny teenagers they felt like they still were.

Noah touched her cheek, drawing her gaze back to his. "Hey. I know you're scared."

When she set her jaw defiantly, he shook his head and rubbed his thumb across her cheekbone. "Don't try to tell me any different. I know you, Emma."

And there it was, right out in the open. He read her like a book. Half of it was stubbornness; resisting on principle alone, and the knowledge that letting herself love him without fear was different than anything she'd done. But the rest of it was fear. She was terrified to turn this momentary happiness into something serious, something tangible that existed outside of themselves that could be bent, broken, or shattered, by themselves or someone else. It was a vulnerability she hadn't allowed herself in her lifetime.

~

Noah waited, holding his breath for something, *anything* from Emma. He knew they'd crossed the body image bridge that first night, and she'd blossomed from anxious about him seeing her without her clothes on to anxious to peel them off for him quicker than he'd expected. He couldn't figure out for the life of him why she still thought there was something wrong with her body when it drove him crazy.

She was avoiding the fundamental issue, the same way she had when she'd holed up in her folks' house before she left for Denver, and he had a feeling this wasn't too different from that, after all. Except that he was in a much different place, now. A place where he could love her the way she deserved, if she'd just let him.

He finally released that breath when she nodded, turning her face into his touch. She was cautious but there was no way she was oblivious to the way their relationship had transformed. He was in deep, and she could wade in the shallow end all she wanted, but she was only lying to herself.

"We can't go back the way we were, can we?"

"Do you want to?" Now that they'd crossed this bridge, exploring new territory together, he knew there was no way in hell they could go back, and he didn't want to.

She lowered her eyes, then brought them back to meet his.

"No."

"Then we'll go through this together, that's all. Like everything else that's happened in our lives. And in the end, we'll have something different than before...but better."

Noah took her face in both of his hands and drew her to him for a kiss. The way she responded under his touch told him that even if she *was* afraid, her heart knew the difference.

"Hey, get a room!" Stephanie called from behind them as she and Jamie emerged, hand in hand, from the woods. It drew the attention of a couple of people nearby and Emma pulled back, flushed with embarrassment. She tried to step away but he wouldn't let her, winding his arm more tightly around her waist. Cindy lifted her head off of Jimmy Sullivan's shoulder directly across from them and gave him a pointed look. He shrugged, tugged Emma to him again and kissed her in a way that should have erased the doubt from everyone's mind, including hers.

TWENTY-FOUR

"CAREFUL," EMMA WARNED Alamo as they skirted around the edge of the fence dividing the ranch properties. As if he understood her, the horse slowed his steps, and Emma was satisfied when she didn't see any new divots in the lawn of the Baylor property. She was running late for Kerri's lesson and had just seen Noah off to help his parents with a load of inventory at the store. He'd been sore; he wanted to see Kerri's first ride on Alamo, but she insisted he would have months to see them together while she was in Denver.

The first indication that she was late was Rex racing across the yard to greet her. He'd come from the porch and she looked up to see Kerri sitting with her elbows on her knees. Normally, she'd have Buckshot ready and warming up in the ring by the time she got there. Her eyes lit up when she saw Alamo and she sprang to her feet.

"Hey Ker. Ready for some speed?"

The teen's smile nearly swallowed her face as she reached them and stroked the gelding's neck. "I'll give it a try."

"You'll do just fine. You just have to be ready for the takeoff. It's a humdinger."

They went to the arena and she helped Kerri mount up on the horse who was considerably taller than her normal mount. She looked completely at home atop him and it settled Emma's heart a bit. Leaving him behind again would be tough, but Kerri was treating riding Alamo akin to meeting a celebrity and she couldn't think of a single person better to take care of him.

She snapped a picture of the pair of them with her phone, feeling like she was marking the beginning of something beautiful, then sent the picture to Noah so he wouldn't feel left out.

"Alright, he's a bit more sensitive than Buckshot, so just make everything you do about half what you would do with Buckshot. Now just try a few figure eights." She nodded and the girl turned the gelding toward the ring. Emma climbed out of the fence and leaned against it from the outside, watching. They would be just fine, she decided within minutes, as Kerri guided the horse with a soft hand and he rewarded her by lowering his head and rounding his back.

"You feel that?" She shouted to Kerri as she felt a body approach beside her. She looked over to see Finn slide up beside her and slip an arm over her shoulders, giving her a friendly squeeze. "Try a serpentine now, straight down the middle. At a walk, first, a couple of times. Really focus on feeling him bend around your leg."

"Hey Champ."

"Hey Finnegan." She smiled at their use of childhood nicknames and snuggled into his side, turning her attention back to the team in the ring. "Like a rubber ball, right? That means he's using his body correctly. You're doing a great job. Try those at a lope now...remember to sit tall so he doesn't leave you behind. Lower that rein hand. Perfect."

Emma smiled again when Kerri tipped forward and squeezed and Alamo adjusted his speed. Once the pair was sufficiently warmed up, Emma climbed into the ring. "Give me a hand, Finn?" She rolled a barrel into the ring and Finn moved up the line fence to the next one, rolling it in under the fence. "You wanna try a pattern?"

"Ohmigod, yes!" Kerri pulled Alamo into the middle of the ring and the horse's ears perked when he saw them slide the third barrel under the fence. Finn paced out the distance while Emma gave Kerri a pep talk.

"Remember what we said about sitting tall. And he likes to go left first."

Kerri raised her eyebrows and Emma remembered that Buckshot, along with about ninety percent of the horses on any circuit, turned right first.

"I know, it's weird. It's my fault we're lefties." She raised her left hand and waved the fingers at the pair. She'd been the only left handed kid in her school, so she'd trained Alamo to turn left for solidarity.

Kerri smoothed her hand over the horse's sooty mane and down his shoulder and it made Emma smile; the boys had turned her into a fine, caring horsewoman.

"And just bring him around at the end. You'll think he's going to run into the fence, but he won't, and once you make that second turn back toward the barrels after you bring him home, he'll just shut off."

Finn waved from the farthest barrel and then headed back to the midway point where Emma had been standing earlier. "Ready?"

Kerri nodded.

"Just let me get back where I was so I can watch it wide screen, in all its glory."

The teen let out a long breath and Emma remembered that nervous feeling the first time she'd opened this horse up on a pattern. She smiled and gave Alamo a pat. "Take care of this girl."

She half-jogged back to the spot where Finn was back outside of the fence, leaning on the rail, and slid out, mirroring his stance. "Okay!"

Kerri tipped her head down, narrowed the barrels in her sights, and sat forward, giving the gelding the cue to start the pattern. As Emma had told her, the horse started left and Kerri, forgetting, nearly got left behind to the right. By the time they rounded the first barrel, she'd straightened herself out and the duo effortlessly turned the second and third barrel, kicking in extra speed to come home. Emma could hear Kerri screeching with uncontrollable laughter as she passed back over the line the first two barrels made and turned him back toward the pattern. The horse geared down to a gentle, bumping jog and Emma smiled, then looked at Finn expectantly.

"Not a bad team," he nodded, impressed.

"Nope. I think this has been my best idea since I came home." She laughed as the team passed by them at the rail. "Give him a few walk rounds and cool him out, Kerri, and then you can put him up in the barn. I'll take him back home tonight but maybe you better get him a more permanent stall ready."

"Definitely your best idea." Finn tipped his head down and his eyes followed the horse. Emma drew her attention away from them long enough to look over at him. The implications of his words tugged at her heart. They hadn't exactly gone official but Finn had to know there was something going on between her and Noah. It took him a minute but he finally turned to look at her.

"What?" she asked.

"I'm not saying getting tangled up with Noah is a *bad* idea..."

Emma flicked her eyes to Kerri, who was patting Alamo's neck and speaking to him as they cooled down. She didn't want to go there with Finn at all, never mind right now, but he had clearly not just come out here to watch Kerri.

"But?"

"But..." He tightened his lips like he was sorry he'd started, and then let out a hiss of air.

"You're a grown woman who can make her own decisions."

"Damn right."

"It's just...you know I love you, Champ, and I'd hate to see anything happen to you. And Noah's a good man, deep down inside...like...deep, deep, like *hard-to-find* deep, sometimes."

She laughed and shoved him playfully in the shoulder. "Knock it off."

Suddenly serious again, Finn swallowed. "Noah has worked hard in the last year, I'll give him that. He was a mess...well, you probably know about that as well as I do."

"I have an idea." After Cutter's party, she wasn't one hundred percent sure that she really knew as much as she thought she did.

"It was bad, real bad, after you left, for a while, but he's straightening out." Finn scuffed his boot against the gravel, much the same way he had when he'd caught Noah kissing her. That day felt a million years and a thousand emotions away, now. "This sounds selfish, but I'm glad you're back if for no other reason than to make sure he doesn't backtrack. I'm tired, Emma."

She looked at Finn and for the first time, she recognized the weariness in his face. He wasn't an old man but she could see lines etched from the grief of losing his wife six months after his brother and sister-in-law. Finn had probably never had time to really mourn for Sunny, because it wasn't long after that Emma had skipped town, and it sounded like he had stepped into her role as Noah's keeper. Guilt was no stranger to her, and she had built her plan for self-preservation by trying to ignore the guilt of leaving Noah alone to fend for himself. She hadn't thought about the other Baylor men and what her departure might have meant to them.

"I'm sorry, Finn."

He shook his head. "Nothing to be sorry for. It wasn't your job. Not mine either. But what do you do when you care about someone who's destroying himself?"

You skip town to save yourself. She reached out and squeezed Finn's shoulder and his countenance brightened a bit.

"Anyways, that's not the only reason I'm glad you're back. We all missed you, Champ. As for Noah, his stories are his own to tell. I'd just hate to have to beat him up for breaking your heart."

Emma laughed. "I don't know what I'd have done if I had any *real* siblings. Three big brothers is about all I can handle. I have a feeling you'd be saying this stuff to me even if it wasn't Noah we were talking about."

Finn gave an 'aw shucks' shrug and twisted his mouth as if considering her words and then nodded. "That's not a lie."

TWENTY-FIVE

"THAT'LL BE KER, won't it?" Ella Baylor came from the back room with a couple of mugs of coffee and set one on the counter in front of Noah. He wasn't that much of a coffee drinker apart from the first morning jolt, but Ella was addicted to the stuff so he humored her and pulled the cup closer. They'd just finished unpacking the weekly inventory run and his phone, which had been laying on the counter, had just dinged a text alert. He looked down at the tiny screen in front of him and at a picture Emma had sent him of Kerri on Alamo and smiled, handing the phone to his mother to take a look.

"Oh would you look at that," Ella smiled, examining the picture for a minute, and then handed the phone back to him. "Did Kerri send that?"

He shook his head. "Emma."

"That Emma." Ella's smile grew and she

shook her head, taking a sip of her coffee before moving to the computer behind the desk to begin keying the delivery into the inventory program.

"What about her?" Noah grinned, leaning against the counter with coffee cup in hand. He could think of a lot of things that went with 'that Emma', but few of them were decent to say in front of his mother. Ella had loved Emma like her own daughter, that was why she'd kept coming back as a kid, and he wondered if her opinion had changed since Emma had gone to Denver.

"She's a sweet girl, and I'm glad she's back in town. It does a heart good to see the two of you together again."

His mother's words were innocent but she tipped a brow up at him as she had another drink of coffee. Everyone sort of knew what was going on but there had been no official announcement and he was reasonably certain if Emma had anything to do with it, there wouldn't be.

"I remember the first time she came over by herself, her mama ten minutes behind her, beside herself scared she'd run off. She just wanted to see if you could come out to play. She was four years old."

Noah smiled. He didn't remember that particular visit but plenty of the ones after, from the first time she'd ridden her pony over the lawn, through his mama's garden, to the time she'd snuck a quart of whiskey out of her daddy's liquor cabinet when they were fourteen. They'd gone to the hay loft and drank the whole thing between them and were sick as dogs the next day.

"Yeah," he said. "I hope she doesn't stay away so long next time."

"You treat her right this time around and maybe she won't." Ella didn't look up from the computer where she'd keyed in a few more numbers.

"What?"

"You think your mama is blind, Noah Baylor?"

"Uh..."

"The correct answer here is 'no ma'am'." She teased, and then finally looked up from the computer screen. "I mighta been born at night, but it wasn't last night. You've loved that girl for a long time and I don't know what the hell you did to drive her out of town for two years, but now that she's back around, I think you might take a lesson or two from your brothers about loving a woman."

He swallowed hard, thinking of Emma at home giving Kerri her riding lesson. She'd never asked for payment, in fact, refused it when Ren had offered, and insisted that the only payment she needed for loaning Alamo was that they took good care of him. She was kind, made an effort to be friendly to everyone and was generous to a fault. She was all the very best parts of him and he'd taken from that. He was the only person he knew who had ever found their way to the end of that generosity. He'd make it right if it killed him.

TWENTY-SIX

EMMA'S CELL BUZZED on her bed and she rolled her eyes, certain it was her manager from Renegade. Now that he knew her daddy was on the mend, he texted her almost daily asking if she knew when she'd be back. She couldn't blame him—she'd left them in a lurch, shorthanded, on short notice, and she had a contract to fulfill. But she wasn't ready to think about going back just yet.

She moved to leave the room and ignore the text, but the phone started ringing and she turned back around to pick it up. There was a text from Noah on the screen and the call was coming from the same place. She swiped her thumb across the screen to answer, laughing.

"You're supposed to give me a minute to type a reply."

"I couldn't wait."

"Patience has never been your strong suit." She smiled. It had been a long time since Noah

Baylor had made her this happy, and she fully intended to follow the advice her daddy had given her at Dane's wedding.

"You're right. Wanna go for a ride? I'm downstairs."

Emma moved to the window and pulled the curtain aside. Noah's truck sat in the driveway and he leaned against the side of it, phone to his ear. He was all lean muscle, and cowboy cool, and it made her giddy. When he saw her, he waved and hit her with a smile that melted her insides in a way that just wasn't decent.

"Do I have a choice here?"

"Not really. Come on down."

She took the steps two at a time, feeling like she was a schoolgirl all over again, the way her stomach rose up in excited butterflies. When she opened the door and stepped out and a smile spread across his face as he caught sight of her, they multiplied. She barely resisted the urge to skip across the driveway into his arms when he opened them for her.

"Hey," she said, feeling shy for just a second. It was strange how that could still happen, though she'd grown considerably more comfortable with the idea that their friendship had evolved into something else.

She stepped into his arms and he pulled her against him, resting both of their bodies back on the hood of his truck. He slid a hand along her shoulder blades and tangled his fingers into the hair at the nape of her neck, pulling her in for a chaste kiss to her forehead.

"Hey," he replied, his voice quiet. They'd seen each other not four hours before, but they'd made an agreement to focus on the ranch work that needed done; Lord knew there was enough of it, during the day and make time for one another in the evenings. It had an added advantage of keeping their little secret from prying family members. There were still stolen kisses and touches here and there; she couldn't keep her hands off him and the feeling seemed to be mutual.

Noah pulled back and rested his forehead against hers for a moment, rubbing the tips of their noses together. Finally, he straightened.

"Let's go, before your ma sees us."

Emma laughed. "They're tucked up in the living room with their coffee and TV."

He laid an exaggeratedly loud, smacking kiss on her lips that had her giggling before they even made contact.

"Alright," she agreed.

Dusk was beginning to settle on the ranches, the light of the day fading. A little chill had crept into the air and in her excitement, she'd forgotten to grab a coat. Wordlessly, Noah pulled his hoodie off and handed it to her. She slid into it and wrapped herself in the scent and warmth of his body that still clung to it. She hugged her arms around herself and inhaled deeply.

"Where're we going?"

That playful smile flitted over his features. "Doesn't matter, does it?"

It really didn't. He led her across the front of the truck and opened the passenger door for her. The shiny chrome of the newly installed running board made the addition stand out and she laughed out loud as she levered herself into the truck.

"When did that happen?"

"This evening," he admitted sheepishly, then closed the door and scooted around the front of the truck. Sliding into the driver's seat, he turned the key in the ignition and the truck roared to life. "I *might* have driven right here after Carter put it on for me. C'mere."

He shifted the pickup into gear, and then laid his arm along the back of the bench seat. Without thinking, she slid into place against his side. He held her close and pressed a kiss to her temple as they pulled out of the yard.

The drive into town was quiet, and comfortable. She watched as the bits and pieces of a lifetime spent in the same small town slid past them in the waning daylight. It was funny that the things she had wanted so badly to escape, framed in a different mindset, could feel so welcoming and wanted. When Noah turned left at the end of the main drag, she knew exactly where they were going and she smiled to herself.

He turned left again on an overgrown two-track goat path into the woods. She knew it well; it was occasionally used in season for a hunting trail but they had gotten more use out of it than anybody, riding through town and stopping at Hinkley's to stuff a couple of sandwiches in their saddle bags before they rode through on their horses. After some time in the thick bush, alders scraping against the sides of the truck, Emma saw a clearing ahead. Noah made a wide arc and backed into it, turning the truck off.

She looked up at him, her lips curving into a smile, and then he reached across them, cupping her jaw in his big hand, tipping her face up so he could press his lips to it. Then, with an expression on his face like an excited little boy, he unbuckled and slid out of the truck. She followed suit. He tipped the seat ahead and produced a couple of plaid blankets, no doubt leftovers from the wedding.

Emma meandered to the end of the truck bed and looked out over the ledge he'd backed up to while he assembled the blankets in the bed of the truck. Three Rivers had earned its name from the confluence of the Colorado and two smaller tributaries. One might have expected rapids and rough water but it was refreshingly quiet where the bodies of water converged. It was beautiful, picturesque, rugged landscape, just miles from town.

"Gosh, I haven't been here in..."

"Forever." Noah had snuck up behind her and wound his arms around her waist, pressing his cheek against hers as they looked out over what they could see of the water with the waning daylight.

She leaned back into him, closing her eyes, and could feel his heart beating against her shoulder blades. This was a place of many deep conversations, heartfelt silences—memories, from a simpler time, before there was any conflict between them at all. When they were just inseparable friends.

"The last time I came here was with you."

"Same here." Noah said in her ear, his warm breath making her skin pebble in goose bumps. He released her all too soon, and climbed into the bed of the truck, offering her a hand to help her up. He arranged the blankets and settled against the back of the truck's cab, opening his arms to her, and she sat in the v made by his legs, her back to his chest. He cocooned the blankets around them and they watched as the sun sank lower.

"Are you trying to tell me you never brought girls here to impress them?" She smiled, thinking of it.

She'd never dated much—too wrapped up in rodeo and ranching—but Noah had almost always had a girl, or one chasing him, until that summer before Gavin died. He'd always still made time for her, and most of those girls found their close friendship unnerving. She'd always found the assumption that there was something going on between her and Noah to be humorous but now she wondered if there hadn't always been something more between them that nobody acknowledged but those girls recognized. The way that, after an absence, her body and mind had responded to him so willingly was a prime indicator of that.

"Never." He ran a hand inside the hoodie, under her t-shirt, resting on her bare stomach, and she resisted the urge to suck it in under his touch. She reminded herself that he knew all the parts of her now; there was no sense in hiding.. "I only came here with you."

"Really?" She craned her neck to look at him, to see if his expression was as serious as his voice sounded and he caught her cheek with his lips.

"Really," he insisted. "This was *our* place. I might not have held too many things sacred, but this was just for us. Even when I made a lot of other shitty decisions after you left, I never brought another girl here."

She processed his words, but his casual touch was distracting as his fingers moved higher, across her ribs, his calloused fingertips brushing the band of her bra. It tickled there and she bowed back into him as if to escape his touch.

"Can I ask you a question, Noah?"

"Anything."

He dropped his lips to the juncture of her neck and shoulder, his response vibrating over skin that was already anxious for his touch. He nicked lightly with his teeth, and then soothed it with his tongue. It was a significant effort to focus on anything but the feel of his hands and mouth on her body.

"How come you never came to Denver?" She drew in a breath, felt his fingers flex against her skin. "I mean, you've talked about how it was a mistake to let me go, but how come you never followed me?"

"You deserved to be happy, sweetheart. I didn't want to stand in the way of that." He lifted his head, resting his chin on her shoulder lightly. Withdrawing his hand from under her shirt, he found her fingers and twisted them into his. "I knew Denver was what you wanted. Lord knows there was enough of me getting what I wanted— what I *thought* I wanted, before you left, but it was never the other way around. I felt sorry for myself for a while, but when I started to sober up, I knew no matter how bad I wanted you, it was your turn to be happy."

More than once in the last couple of weeks, she had considered what it was she had actually wanted then. It had been unfathomable to move on to a life that had no Noah in it at all, but she had done it. She'd thought the empty ache she filled with her work at Renegade was just missing the family she'd left behind.

"You know that feeling like when you want something your whole life, and you just think if you can get that thing, your whole life will be better?"

"Is that me?"

She couldn't tell if he was joking or serious, but she let out her next breath in a rush.

"That's Denver."

He squeezed her fingers and she felt his cheek swell with a smile beside her.

"Em, I messed up a lot. A lot more than you were around to see. But when Finn finally knocked some sense into me, all I could think about was making myself into the type of man you would deserve—even if you never came back. And now here you are, and you're willing to have me. I wanna pinch myself every other day or so, just to make sure it's real."

His words made her smile. If she was honest with herself, she'd never felt so earnestly wanted. The truth was Noah was the man she wanted, regardless. She didn't know what to do with the idea that he'd spent so much time trying to shape himself into someone she would want, but it warmed her. He'd had issues he needed to deal with, but the fundamentals of the man she knew was exactly what she wanted.

She rose up on her knees, turning to face him. His hands slid to her hips and she circled his neck with her arms.

"Oh, it's real, cowboy."

~

Noah took in a sharp breath before Emma drew her mouth down to his. He tightened his arms around her waist and pulled her flush to him, changing the angle and intensity of the kiss as he took the lead away from her. Guiding her without breaking the kiss, he shifted her knees to the outsides of his thighs and settled her into his lap, sliding his hands into the back pockets of her jeans and pulling her snug against him.

Her softness melted into his hardness and

she molded herself around his body, drawing a groan from deep in his chest. His intent bringing her out here had been one hundred percent innocent, but the taste of her made it damn hard to remember that.

"I swear to Jesus, if you go back to Denver, I'll follow you. I'd follow you to the ends of the earth." She rocked her hips against his and he thought he might come in his jeans. Breaking the kiss to tug the hoodie over her head, he was delighted to see her t-shirt go with it, leaving her in nothing but a wine colored bra with delicate scalloped lace on the edges. He tugged the blankets tighter around her shoulders and pressed his mouth against the little hollow at the top of her sternum, then grazed the stubble of his jaw down across the sexy little valley between her breasts. She bowed forward into him this time—just the result he was looking for—and a soft noise came from her as she fisted her fingers into his hair. He pressed his face into the cleavage that presented itself then, inhaling the essence of her. Tipping his face up, he caught the skin over the delicate pulse in her throat with his teeth, then his lips, then drew. Her fingers corresponded, tightening.

"I don't want to think about Denver right now." She ground the words out, the timbre of her voice low and needy, sending a pulse of desire straight to the spot where their bodies pressed together. He cursed the two layers of denim separating them when all he wanted to do was sink into her and stay there. "I want to think about you.

And me. And this."

To punctuate her words, she rolled her hips, pushing against him. He drew another tight breath, his head dropping back against the back window of the truck's cab.

"Sweetheart, you keep that up..."

The wickedest little grin tipped the corners of her lips up. He'd always figured he knew every facet of her personality but he was discovering more every day, and they were all pleasant, teasing surprises like this.

"Keep *what* up?" She moved again and he surged forward, bending his knees and pushing her onto her back as they traded positions. She screeched at the movement and kept her hands cinched around his neck, laughing as he kneeled between her legs and then fell forward onto his hands, hovering over her. Without a word, and with precision he hadn't expected, she unbuttoned his jeans, and slipped a hand inside to cradle him. His hips pushed into her hand almost on their own accord, and a groan rumbled from his chest.

"You're way too naughty for your own good," he murmured as he dusted his lips across her jaw, behind her ear, over her collarbone.

"Oh yeah? What are you gonna do about it?" She chuckled as her fingers threaded through his hair, keeping his mouth close as he traveled down to the front clasp in her bra, using one hand to pop it open. Quickly, he drew one nipple between his teeth, scraping his teeth gently along her sensitive skin. Her body jolted and she drew in a quick breath, but arched her back, pushing up into his mouth. God, the way she reacted to him was so damn hot.

"I'll show you." Loathe to move out of her reach, he shifted lower, trailing the gentlest of damp kisses along her exposed skin, moving South. With his tongue at her navel, he unsnapped her jeans, and then broke the contact to jerk them down her hips roughly.

He touched his lips to the inside of her knee, and moved up her thigh, stopping to look up and catch her eyes. They were smoldering and wanting, and more than that, they were trusting. She had no idea—no idea at all how badly he wanted her. It was all he could do sometimes not to push her up against the wall of the barn in the middle of the morning feed. She deserved more than a truck bed on a chilly fall night, and he intended to give that to her every day for the rest of their lives, but for now...

She tucked her lower lip between her teeth and nodded to him and he lowered his mouth to her center and tasted her. He felt her whole body tense when he made contact and he lifted his head to check with her again. The realization of what the look in her eyes meant burned in his chest. Nobody had ever bothered to love her like this, or she just hadn't let them. He kicked himself for not having gotten to it sooner.

"You okay, sweetheart?"

She let out a pent up breath and then nodded. He felt her body relax minutely and he touched his mouth to her again. She wriggled under his touch, like she might try to get away and he slid his arms under her thighs to hold her hips still. The humming noise that came out of her next was sexy as hell, and it was about all he could do not to lose himself in her softness.

Before long, her hips rose to his touch and he felt her fingers curling in his hair. A tremor moved through her body and short breaths hiccupped out of her. He reached up and caught one of her hands, tangling his fingers into hers just as his name came out of her, a low moan. She shuddered twice and came apart, his name tumbling off her lips.

TWENTY-SEVEN

IT TOOK MORE than a minute for Emma to catch
her breath. She laid on her back with the blankets
pulled up to her chin, letting out long, slow breaths
to center herself.

"Oh God." She sighed the words as much as
said them.

Noah leaned up on one elbow and splayed
his hand across her belly, igniting a little fire. Her
jeans were still undone and halfway down her hips
and she had no idea where her shirt had gone to
and didn't give a damn. He'd rocked the hell out of
her world; she couldn't have moved if she'd wanted
to.

"Sweetheart, we are just getting started."

Blue lights flickered across the sky and it
took Emma a moment to realize they weren't a part
of her fragmented reality.

"Oh my God, Noah."

"I know," he murmured, his lips traveling

across her jaw.

"No, Noah." *Oh God*...Her voice barely above a whisper, she pulled the blanket up higher and wished she could pull it clear over her head and disappear through the bed of the truck. "I think the sheriff is here."

"Shit." Noah scrambled onto his knees, buttoning up his jeans in a hurry. "Shit, it's Banks."

Paralyzed with embarrassment, she laid on her back in the bed of the truck as she heard a car door close and boots crunching across gravel. Noah stood.

"Evening, sheriff."

"Noah, what the hell are you doing out here all alone?"

She heard Noah cough and footsteps approaching, then saw uniformed arms fold over the edge of the truck bed as Banks peered down at her.

"Not alone, I guess. Evening, Emma." The sheriff's face betrayed his casual tone but he quickly rearranged his features to hide his surprise at finding her in her current state of undress.

If she could have melted into the floor or thrown herself into the river, she would have. She pressed her cool fingers to her inflamed face. She was so embarrassed she could cry; they were worse than a pair of horny teenagers. They should have known better.

"Can I help you, Banks?" Noah perched on the cab of the truck, crossing his arms over his chest, no doubt an attempt to be as casual as he could.

"Oh, no, this was just my normal check. We usually dig a few underage drinkers a week out of here. Usually one of those Sullivan kids."

An awkward silence stretched out between the three of them. Banks clearly wished he'd found a Sullivan instead of a Baylor and a Pierce.

Finally, Noah spoke. "Well, no liquor here, and we're all of age." He ran a hand through his hair, scuffing his boot on the bed of the truck. He must have been nervous; Lord knew she was.

"Figure you two might as well head on home, though." Banks nodded, his voice wavering when he passed his eyes to Emma. "You wanna get on outta there, Emma?"

She heard Noah's boot scuff on the truck bed again and realized he had pushed the hoodie and t-shirt across to her so she could dress herself. She slid up into a sitting position, still covering herself with the blanket. If he could have just left them there, it would have been great, but she knew he was just doing his due diligence.

"Would you mind turning around, Banks?"

Clearly a little embarrassed, he coughed and slowly turned to face in the other direction, his hands on his hips. As quickly as she could, she pulled the sweater over her head and wriggled her jeans up her hips, zipping up the fly. She was certain, judging by the hot flush clinging to her cheeks—a combination of the mind-blowing orgasm she'd just had, and the embarrassment—that she was the color of a tomato.

Noah swung both legs over the edge of the truck bed and landed on the gravel, holding his arms out for her and she first sat with her legs hanging over the side of the truck, then slid onto legs that barely supported her. Noah steadied her with hands on her hips and, without a word, pressed a kiss to her lips. Banks turned back around, a relieved smile crossing his features. He was clearly considerably more comfortable when everyone had all their clothes *on*. She was, too.

Noah retrieved the blankets from the bed of the truck and opened his driver's side door to stuff them behind the seat.

"Sorry for the bother, Sheriff," Noah said, as he sidled up beside Emma.

"Oh, it's no bother. I'm just glad I'm not dragging you down to the station."

Emma knew Banks was referencing the kids he normally pulled out of here but she felt Noah stiffen beside her. She supposed that period of his life would always be a sore spot. The sheriff seemed to recognize his gaffe and shifted uncomfortably. Considering how incredible she had felt just before Banks showed up, there was a hell of a lot of discomfort going around.

She drew in a deep breath, breaking the silence, anxious to vacate the uncomfortable scene. "Okay, well, we should be going. Good to see you again, Banks."

She took Noah's arm and guided him toward his open driver's door, then walked around the hood of the truck, hoping her wobbly gait wasn't too obvious.

The sheriff tipped his hat as they climbed into the truck but didn't get into his car until Noah had put the truck in gear and started to pull out.

"Oh my God," she mumbled, covering her face with both hands, and sinking down in the passenger seat.

Noah was quiet, too quiet – pissed off, maybe? She uncovered her eyes and looked over. He was bent over the steering wheel, his shoulders shaking with silent laughter.

She crossed her arms, frowning at him, and waited until he could get a word out.

"The look on your face, Em." He wiped a tear from the corner of his eye, his breath still coming in gasps. "I thought you were gonna die right there."

"That was *so* not funny, Noah Baylor."

"It was—for all the times I've gone parking, I've never been caught. Not until I was twenty six years old with someone I actually gave a damn about. And shit, did you see Banks' face?"

He giggled at the mention of Banks and it wasn't manly or sexy, but it was infectious and Emma caught it, thinking of the sheriff's embarrassed red face.

Noah put on his blinker as he turned out of the dirt lane and headed back toward town. He watched in his rear view mirror until Banks turned off behind them and then increased his speed. He practically spit up dirt as they pulled into a driveway that she didn't immediately recognize. It wasn't until he shut off the ignition that she remembered being here the night she'd been at Danny's. She cast her eyes to him questioningly, though the thought of being alone, without worrying about who saw what or sneaking in and out of windows answered any question she might have.

"I'm done feeling like I'm seventeen all over again." His voice was low and whatever had relaxed after he'd made her come pulled deep in her belly. Everything inside of her turned molten and she let out a tight breath. There was a promise in his words that she couldn't wait to fulfill.

They sprinted from the truck to the house, still high on the adrenaline of having been caught by Banks. Noah kicked the door shut behind them and then pushed her against it, hands trapping hers as he buried his face in her neck, inhaling deeply.

A clash of hands and clothes, mouths and flesh led them to the bedroom. The same bedroom where he'd turned her drunken advances down just a few weeks earlier. Now, he couldn't seem to get her undressed fast enough, and she didn't need an ounce of liquor to want him to. He tugged the hoodie and t-shirt up again, breaking the kiss only long enough to pull it over her head. They stepped out of jeans and shoes and socks and never stopped touching one another. As they got closer to the bed, his urgent hands stilled and he held her at arm's length. She could feel his eyes as if they were an actual touch, roaming over her body.

It still felt strange when he looked at her

like this. Proprietary, hungry, dark with desire. And because she knew exactly what sort of reactions he could coax out of her when he had that look on his face, her knees weakened. She grabbed his shoulders just a second before he pushed her back onto the bed and they tumbled into it in a tangle of limbs.

Laughter bubbled out of her as she felt his weight cover her, and then the sensation of turning as he wrapped his arms around her and rolled onto his back so their positions were reversed. The instinct to wriggle out of the position as gracefully as she could was strong—she was too heavy for this—but he held her in place, pressing a kiss to her forehead.

"Let's try this without our clothes on." He spoke with a grin, sliding his hands down her sides to frame her hips, guiding her into an upright position and sliding her forward to join their bodies in one fluid movement. She braced with her hands on his chest, her lower lip tucked between her teeth, and any worries she had been hanging onto slipped out of her head with the guttural groan that came out of him.

Experimentally, she tipped her hips against him like she had in the bed of the truck and he made another noise, deeper than the last. This new angle lit up pleasure centers she hadn't even known existed and she rocked against him to make it last. His hands slid from her hips to cup her heavy breasts and back down again as she found an easy rhythm against his hard body.

Too soon, and before she was ready, Emma felt herself rising toward another orgasm. She slowed, furrowing her brow and a wicked grin spread across Noah's features as he slid a hand between them, touching her at the spot where their bodies joined and tipped her over the edge.

TWENTY-EIGHT

NOAH TRACED A finger along the curve of Emma's shoulder, marveling at the softness of her skin. The sun had started to filter in through his bedroom window and cast a wedge of gold light across the back of her head and shoulders. She laid on her stomach with the sheets around her waist. Her face was peaceful, relaxed in her slumber, and breathtakingly beautiful. It had taken him far too long to let himself see Emma this way.

He was awake before his alarm—an incredible feat if he'd ever heard of one—but he had a load on his mind. It was too damn early, and the last thing he wanted to do was get out of this bed and go to the barn, but he knew he didn't have any other choice.

She moved a little and when she opened her eyes, she smiled a smile that was like a shot to the heart.

"Hey," her voice was husky with sleep.

"Hey." He smiled back at her and slid his palm over her shoulder.

"What time is it?"

"We still have a few minutes." He tipped forward and pressed his lips to the curve his fingers had been tracing just moments before. "Take your time."

"How long have you been awake?" She shifted, pushing her hair back from her face and tucking her hands under her cheek.

"Just a little bit. I was thinking about Denver."

She groaned plaintively and closed her eyes. "I told you I don't want to think about Denver right now."

"I know, but we gotta think about it, Em. It's getting close."

She grumbled again but didn't reply.

"I want you to go," he continued. Now that he had her in his life this way, he couldn't imagine what it would be like to send her away again, to not be able to step over the snake rail fence and see her whenever he wanted. No, the selfish parts of him didn't *want* her to go, but the rest of him recognized that it was the best thing for her to do at this point. To erase any doubts in her mind that he only wanted her because she was there, and always had been. To let her feel the satisfaction of finishing what she'd started. To allow her to want to hopefully come home to Three Rivers to settle, though he'd have followed her to the ends of the earth.

Her eyes shot open and she lifted her head. "You want me to go?"

"When your daddy is ready. Finish out the contract, don't burn any bridges. It's only a couple of hours away. I'll visit on the weekend. When it's over, you can come back here, or we can go somewhere else. Whatever you want to do."

"You'd leave Three Rivers?"

"Sweetheart, my home is here, but my heart is wherever you are. A man can't live without his heart."

"You lived for two years without it." Despite the soberness of the statement, her tone teased. She wiggled into a sitting position, tugging the sheet across her lap as she sat cross legged on the bed in front of him, her navel at eye level – she was staring him down, but he couldn't take his eyes off her exposed body.

Her words made his heart twist up in his chest.

"That wasn't living. Not compared to this...you in my bed, in my arms, in my bloodstream. It's like I'm drunk all over again—the good kind—but there's no whiskey involved."

Wordlessly, she leaned over him, brushing her lips across his. He tugged her close, pressing his fingers into the yielding flesh at her hip. When she pulled away, he lifted his head to chase the kiss, tugging his teeth across her lower lip gently. With a hand on his chest, she pushed him back down to the bed. Despite his best efforts to the contrary, the sheets tented at his waist.

The movement drew her eyes and she arched a brow. She licked her lips and he didn't know if she did it on purpose or not, but he knew then if they didn't leave this bed *right now*, they wouldn't at all.

He rolled onto his back to distract himself from the desire he had to reach out and run his hands over all that bare skin. If he had the time, he'd *show* her that he'd follow her to the ends of the earth if that was what it took. He tucked his hands under his head and looked at the ceiling, breathing a sigh of relief when his alarm finally blared. Jonas could excuse oversleeping, but he wasn't sure how well that would go over when he found out Noah had overslept *with his daughter*.

"We've got to get going," she said, finally tearing her eyes from him.

"It's amazing what a morning person you've become under the right circumstances." He grinned, watching her as she slid off the bed.

"Well you didn't know that yet. You were taking your life in your hands waking me up there, friend." She laughed, discarding the sheet though she kept her back to him as she gathered her clothes from the floor. Someday, he hoped she'd feel more comfortable, but for now, he was appreciating the view of the curves of her body in the morning light. He made no move to get up.

"Come on, Noah. We've got to get a move on." She finally turned and saw him reclined, watching her. "What?"

"You look like an angel, with your hair all

messy and the sunlight coming in." He smiled when she rolled her eyes exaggeratedly at him. "And I love you, Emma Pierce."

~

Emma froze in her tracks, holding her jeans and his hoodie in front of her naked body; the rest of her clothes were still scattered across the floor. Her heart pounded in her ears like a stampede, and her mouth went dry. She wanted desperately to say something, anything, but she couldn't form any words. Her stomach seized up, a feeling of dread entirely like the last time he'd said these words. This was different, of course. He'd just told her to go back to Denver, finish out what she had originally thought was her dream—the complete opposite of the last time when he'd wanted her to stay.

She'd surrendered her body and her heart to him, but those three words felt like the last grip she had on reality. They felt like letting go of the control she'd spent two years away from home trying to develop.

"You don't gotta say it back." Finally, he unfolded his hands from behind his head and moved to get out of the bed, letting the sheet fall away from his body—that body she couldn't actually believe fit to hers so well—and casually pulled on his jeans from the day before, with nothing underneath. "But you should know. I've meant it since the first time I tried to tell you, at least.

Maybe longer. Before I was smart enough to tell you. And now that I've smartened up, there's no way in hell I'm letting the opportunity get past me again."

He found her underwear near the nightstand at the head of the bed and handed them to her, kissing her unmoving lips when he approached. He seemed barely affected by her silence.

"Come on, let's go. We've got time for breakfast at Hinkley's if we move our asses."

With the feel of his warm lips on hers, Emma's heart finally started moving blood through her body again. She fumbled into her clothes and followed him out of the bedroom.

The drive to the diner was just a couple of blocks, and mostly silent, but when he shifted his truck into park at the curb in front of Hinkley's, Noah finally spoke, with a playful smile on his lips.

"You can stop looking at me like that."

She carefully schooled her features into what she hoped looked like a normal face and tipped her head toward him. "Like what?"

"Like a deer in the headlights. The only thing this changes is that you go to Denver knowing that I *love* you." He grinned when he said this time, like he couldn't be any prouder of the revelation. "Sounds good, doesn't it?"

It *did* sound good. Maybe too good to be true.

TWENTY-NINE

"YOU READY?" EMMA turned to her father in the passenger's seat of her tiny car.

"I'm gonna tell them to put me on disability so I can keep you here." Even though he was teasing, he could have been half serious; she wouldn't have put it past him.

Rolling her eyes, she laughed. "Oh come on, now. I'm not afraid of Three Rivers anymore, I'll come home for holidays."

Jonas let out a big, exaggerated huff and pushed the door open. "Alright, let's get this rolling, if we gotta."

Following her father into the clinic, Emma held in a breath and then let it go in one long rush. This could be her ticket back to Denver. Today. She could leave tomorrow, her manager would expect her to. At the end of the day, it was a job, and it paid better than Hinkley's. She didn't have any excuses not to come home to visit anymore, either.

It didn't have to be the way it had been before she'd come home.

As she stepped through the door that her father held open for her, Emma was hit with a rush of air conditioning. The office was empty; they were the last appointment of the day. She smiled at Layla Sullivan sitting behind the receptionist's desk. Layla was a tall girl, like Emma. Blond and blue eyed, and what Emma could only describe as rugged—the same descriptor she used for herself. They could have been cousins.

"I didn't know you worked here, Layla."

The girl smiled back. The Baylor brothers had always had one problem or another with the Sullivan boys but Layla had always been decent. She was a sweet, shy girl who had never hurt anyone. If Emma had to guess, she supposed the brash, brazen boys she'd grown up with had put a good damper on her.

"You can go right in, Mr. Pierce. Dr. Fields is ready for you."

"How many times have I got to tell you to call me Jonas, Layla?"

Layla blushed as he walked by the desk and through the partially opened door to the doctor's office; Jonas' particular brand of teasing charm clearly still took her by surprise. Emma took a seat and pulled out her phone as it buzzed. More often than not these days, she'd been leaving it in her bedroom while she worked around the ranch— partly to avoid the distraction and partly to avoid the texts from her manager, which had increased in frequency, knowing this day was coming. Sure enough, it was her manager, Craig, looking for an update.

Holding the phone in both hands, she squeezed her arms between her knees, drew a breath into her cheeks, and let out slowly. She saw Layla look up. Nervous butterflies flittered in her stomach and she sat back, trying to calm them.

The chair she'd been sitting in scraped noisily as she rose to her feet. Her father turned in the door of the doctor's office and raised a brow. Shoving her phone in her pocket, she moved for the door.

"I'm just going to take a walk over to Hinkley's for a coffee, Daddy."

"Okay, sweetie. I'll come find you."

Emma pushed out into the clear brightness of the day and paused, giving herself a chance to center before she walked away. It was surprising how, thinking about going back to Denver, she realized how much she loved Three Rivers and could see herself here all over again. And if she thought about it, it wasn't entirely Noah's fault, either, though it certainly factored in. Sometimes all one needed was a step away to appreciate what they had in front of them.

Hands in her pockets, she walked along the store fronts between Dr. Fields' office and the diner. There was the bakery, Sawyer's grocery, Danny's across the street. Each business represented a hard working face she had known her whole life. She smiled at Tina as she slipped into Hinkley's. The older waitress was on alone; most weekday afternoons weren't terribly busy, but there were still a number of patrons she recognized from her days serving. She nodded and waved at the Robinsons, a couple of her regulars and seated herself at the counter.

"What can I get for ya, honey?" Tina asked as she sidled up to the counter with a coffee pot in hand. Emma turned the clean mug that had been sitting in front of her right side up and watched as her long-time friend filled it with steaming coffee.

She would miss this. Tina, and Hinkley's, and a good cup of coffee. If her daddy hadn't always taught her to finish what she started, she might have called the whole thing off. But there were people in Denver who were counting on her. Craig and Allison were just the tip of the iceberg.

"And a piece of banana cream pie?" Tina offered, tipping her head toward the display case. "It's super fresh."

Emma smiled and nodded in return. "You know me way too well."

"Well, you haven't had a piece since you came home." The waitress busied herself with getting the slice of pie and leaned close as she set it down in front of Emma. "And word on the street is that you're probably heading out again, soon."

She didn't bother to ask how Tina would have come across that information. The diner was practically the hub of the rumor mill in town, and maybe that was why Emma was so adverse to gossip, because she'd heard so much of it.

"Daddy's getting checked out now. He could be cleared to go back to work on the ranch today."

Tina clucked her tongue and shook her head. "Well, I'll be awful sorry to see you go. You let me know if you need anything else."

With that, the woman, who never seemed to stop moving, took off to collect dishes off a table. Emma heard the tinkle of the bell at the door but didn't look up. The pie was more or less the best thing Hinkley's served—real bananas, the best flakey, homemade crust, and thick cream. It was an indulgence she rarely partook of and she hardly noticed when someone sat beside her at the counter.

"Emma Pierce. I heard you were back in town."

Even now, Emma would have recognized Jimmy Sullivan's voice anywhere. She frowned and looked up. She'd never had a problem with Jimmy, but she'd stood between him and Noah enough times that he disliked her by default. She had too much of an opinion, he'd told her once, for a woman.

"Jimmy." She nodded in greeting, because it was the polite thing to do, and turned back to her pie, wishing she could rewind a few minutes and be alone with it again.

"Heard you were hanging out with Noah Baylor again." He shifted forward on his elbows on the counter and nodded to Tina. "I'll have the same as her. Pie and coffee."

She looked back up, narrowing the man in her gaze as Tina filled his coffee cup. "What can I do for you, Jimmy?"

"Just being neighborly. That outlawed in Denver?" He shook his head and lifted his coffee mug to his lips, but he had her hooked now. Since when did Jimmy Sullivan give two shits about being neighborly? The contrast of his sister's sweet gentleness and his rough, brash attitude was all too evident.

She rolled her eyes and turned back to the pie, cutting a large piece off with her fork, determined to head back to Dr. Fields' office as quickly as possible. Sitting there, listening to canned Muzak and reading an eight month old copy of *Health News Today* sounded like a Caribbean holiday compared to keeping this company for a second longer.

"I just don't know what a good girl like you sees in a shit stain like him."

Her spine stiffened and she looked back at him, certain she wasn't going to like the direction this was headed.

"What are you after, Jimmy?"

"I'd just hate to see you hurt, right when you're getting your life in order in Denver. Makin' it big with the jackpot races, I heard."

He'd heard wrong, but she didn't correct him. He clearly had something to say and she'd lost her appetite. She wiped her mouth with a napkin and got up, dropping a ten dollar bill and tapping the counter to get Tina's attention. "Keep the change, Tina."

"Don't let me run you off, Emma. Just be careful who you keep company with. That piece of shit knocked Layla up and didn't stand by her when she lost it. Sounds like a good, respectable member of the community to me." Jimmy sucked his tongue across his top teeth and took another sip of his coffee, unaffected by the bomb he'd just dropped on Emma.

Emma, on the other hand, fought the urge to vomit and run, and nodded her goodbye to Tina, doing her best to exit the diner at an unhurried pace. Noah had done some shitty things under the influence of alcohol and grief, she knew that much. And Jimmy was known to stretch the truth more than a little, especially when it was advantageous to him. She couldn't figure what the advantage here would be, but she could do her best to chalk it up to bad blood and not truth.

Still...she *had* seen Noah out of control more than once before she'd left for Denver. He hadn't mentioned any kind of relationship with Layla. And she didn't know anything about the time between when she'd left and when she'd come back, only that he'd somehow unstuck his life and gotten sober.

Suddenly, the conversation she'd had with Finn came back to her, seeming less casual than it had actually been. *His stories are his own to tell...* Was this a story he just hadn't told her yet? Like Cindy Warden. She hated doubting him, and she knew it was her own fault she didn't know these things; her policy that ignorance was bliss was coming to bite her in the ass.

Her stomach churning, Emma dragged her feet as she walked back to Dr. Fields' office, resentful that something she'd been enjoying so much had been soured by Jimmy, and anxious about seeing Layla.

The girl looked up and smiled as she pulled the door open again. Emma gave her the longest look she could without being obvious. She wasn't sure what she was expecting to see; there was no evidence of any pregnancy, there wouldn't have been. Jimmy had said she'd lost it. But when? How long had she been pregnant? Had Noah made plans to make her an honest woman? She might have come home to a much different scene.

While Emma did her best to paste something better than a grimace on numb features, Layla twisted her long braid between her fingers and offered her a warm smile.

"Welcome back."

"Thanks." It was all she could do not to jump on the girl and ask a thousand questions, and she just might have if her father's large hand hadn't clapped down on her shoulder, startling her. She turned and saw his supportive sling was gone and he had a sad smile on his face.

"Dr. Fields just cleared me for work. Guess it's time for you to go back to your fancy racing team?"

Emma swallowed, desperately trying to keep herself on an even keel. It was all a lot to process and she felt like she'd been hit by a Mac truck. She passed a brief smile to Dr. Fields, Layla and finally to her father.

"I guess so. Soon." She barely knew what she was saying, just that she needed to get out of this office, and to the bottom of this rumor. She should have been happy for her father's news, but she couldn't stop thinking about Jimmy Sullivan's words.

"Let's go home and tell your mother." He squeezed her shoulder lightly, guiding her toward the door. He cleared his throat and when Emma looked up, she didn't see the smile that she thought she should have.

In the parking lot, her father stopped at the door of the car, and looked at Emma over the roof for a long moment. Had he known? Had everyone known about Noah and Layla but her?

"You promise you'll come back for Christmas, right?"

"Daddy, stop being so silly. You know I'll be here. Denver is only two hours." Right now, it felt like just enough space to breathe.

"Yeah, that's what you said the first time."

As if she could feel any more anxiety and pain, her father's words pierced her heart. All the pressure made her feel as if it could burst at any second. As she slid into the driver's seat of her car, her limbs felt slow and loaded with ice. Her palms were clammy and her fingers numb. Nonetheless, she guided the car home, the silence between her and her father stretching long and tense until they pulled into the driveway.

Myrna was sitting on the porch in a rocker, enjoying the last sun of the afternoon, waiting for them. She stood when she saw them pull in, a broad smile across her face.

Jonas rolled down his window and swung his arm in a big waving motion, the tension of the drive seemingly gone from his mind.

"Ma! It's a miracle, I'm healed!"

Her mother laughed as Emma parked the car and Jonas jumped out to dance a little jig.

"I told you that physical therapy wasn't a waste of time." Emma's mother folded her father into a warm hug and he lifted her hand over her head and gave her a twirl before tugging her close to sway their bodies to music that Emma couldn't hear.

"Em." A shard of ice went straight up Emma's spine when she heard Noah's voice. "You wanna give me a hand in the barn?"

She didn't reply right away, heard Noah chuckle at her parents' antics, and then he tried again. "Earth to Em?"

"Yeah." She turned to look at him, taking in his tall, broad figure, his hat in his hands. She saw him in a different light, now. Not just the Noah who had been selfish and hurt *her*, but the Noah who had left a path of destruction in his wake. Not just before she'd left, but well after, too.

"Oh, Noah, I'll give you a hand." Jonas made to release his wife.

"Oh no, Jonas. You two keep up your

celebrating. There will be plenty of time for you to throw hay and feed stock."

Noah raised an eyebrow in invitation to Emma and turned toward the barn and she followed, still numb.

Once they'd cleared the door of the barn, Noah tugged her to the side, into his arms. His mouth found her throat and she melted almost immediately, her body responding to his in a way that her mind couldn't give in to. He pinned her against the wall and a shiver of excitement ran up her spine, the overpowering sandalwood and leather smell of him intoxicating. Suddenly, hot blood was running through her veins again and she slipped her fingers into his belt loops and jerked his hips against her tightly.

He groaned against her neck and scraped his teeth along the soft skin there, his stubble tickling and sending skittering sensations across the surface of her flesh. His fingers found their way under the hem of her shirt and slid upward, splaying his work-roughened palms over her ribcage and sneaking higher still.

"Do you have any idea how badly I want you?" His breath was hot against her skin and the sensation of cool air hitting that spot made her shudder, sliding a hand up between his shoulder blades and pressing him tighter. "The thought of you going to Denver makes it worse. I was so distracted, it took me ten minutes to remember how to start the tractor this morning."

She whimpered as his lips moved lower. He

tugged at the neck of her shirt, popping a couple of buttons open so his tongue could trace the line of her collarbone. Her head fell back against the wall, knocking as it made contact, the buzz of anticipation making her short circuit to the point where she almost couldn't think...until Layla Sullivan's face showed up in her mind. It was a reminder that this was all too consuming, too fast, too deep. There were still things she didn't know. Things he hadn't told her.

"Noah...Noah." She released the pressure between his shoulder blades and moved her hand to his chest. He'd worked his way back up across her jawline and sucked her earlobe into his mouth. "We have to talk."

"There's all kinds of time for talking, Em. Texting and phone calls. But we're not gonna have much time for this sort of thing."

"No, Noah." She pressed her hand to his chest a little more firmly and he finally lifted his head, his dark eyes searching hers. "We need to talk before I go. We need to talk about Layla Sullivan."

~

You're a big asshole, Noah Baylor. The minute she said Layla's name, Noah's heart stopped. Somewhere in the back of his mind, especially after Cutter's party, Noah had known this was a bridge he needed to cross. He just hadn't found the right time or words, and he had a hard time focusing on much but Emma these days. It was too late now to do the right thing.

"What about Layla Sullivan?" He knew what was coming but he led her anyways. She looked like she wanted to walk away but he'd moved his hands to her waist, his fingers twisted in her shirt to hold her in place. If he let her go, she could fly away. She'd already done it once before.

"Why didn't you tell me?"

"I was waiting for the right time, Em."

"It's pretty important, Noah."

"Who even told you about me and Layla?"

"Does it matter, Noah? It's true, right? So you should have told me."

There was anger in her eyes—*that* he could handle. What he couldn't handle, and hadn't expected, was the hurt on her face. It was so reminiscent of two years before that if he'd known it would be this way, he would have rewound back to the first day she'd come home and let the events with Layla be the first thing he'd told her. That way there would have been nothing to destroy with this pain, or they could have built beyond it.

"You've hardly been here long enough for us to get used to each another again, Em. What was I supposed to say 'welcome home, and by the way, I was completely out of my mind after you left and I fucked up other people's lives, too'?"

Her chest rose and fell with the shallow breaths she drew through her half opened mouth. Her stricken eyes watched him as he took a step back, untwisted his hands from the fabric of her shirt and ran them through his hair roughly. This was a nightmare, played over and over every time he saw Layla, but he couldn't go back in time and change anything. He could only try to be better. Emma made him better. And he'd screwed her over yet again.

"I don't know." Her voice was tiny and quiet. "I don't know, Noah, but you should have told me."

"I'll tell you now." He'd give her a minute-by-minute run down of the last two years if it could erase that hurt look in her eyes and the defeated slump in her shoulders.

"Okay."

"I hurt people, Emma. I hurt *you*. It's not something I'm proud of or that I want to relive all the time. I made mistakes and I've done my best to fix them the best way I know how."

He paced a few short steps away and then turned back. His fear was real; he could barely hear himself think over the rushing of blood in his ears. He didn't know what he would do if she ran like she had two years ago. This was different; he was so wrapped up in her now that it might kill him to lose her again.

"You want to know the truth? It was worse after you left than before. That's on me. I can't blame you for trying to get away from all of this." He gestured to himself. "I knew nobody could replace you, but I tried. For a few months. Layla...she was just in the wrong place at the wrong time."

He shook his head and wiped a hand over

his face. "It wasn't supposed to happen that way. We got together a few times and then all of a sudden, she's telling me there's to be a baby and she's got this look on her face like the best thing in the world has happened to her and all I can think is if this is real, I can't even pretend that someday you and I would have a future."

In the end, it *had* all come back to Emma. He would have done the right thing by Layla...eventually, at Finn's prompting, but he would have mourned for Emma.

"She showed up one night, knocking on the door. She was losing it and I'd been drinking all day. I couldn't get out of bed, never mind drive her to the hospital. Finn took her and when he came back, he socked me in the face and told me to get myself under control. So I fixed what I could. But there are some things you can't just fix without some time. And that's my burden to bear, not yours."

He heard a big breath come rushing out of her. This was the last thing he'd wanted—to hurt her again. After they'd made all this progress, after they'd come so far.

"I wish it had never happened. I wish I had done something before it got that bad. I should have just come to see you in Denver...but I thought the best thing for you was to let you have the life you wanted, away from Three Rivers, without my interference. You were smart to walk away from me. I was a piece of shit then, and I had nothing to offer you or anybody else but hurt."

Her face was flushed and he could see unshed tears behind her eyes. He hated the distance between them, wanted to take two steps to her and hold her in his arms. He wanted to promise he'd never make her cry again, but it all seemed to fall short. She was quiet, and she'd closed her mouth. Her jaw worked the way that it did when she was thinking hard about something. And he prayed, like he had never done before.

"Em, please say something."

She swallowed and straightened, lifting her weight off of the wall of the barn. The silence stretched between them so long and deep he could feel every thud of his heart, every pulse of blood through his veins. Agonizing. She was poised to go back to Denver and he'd made all of this headway only to lose her again because he'd been stupid, trying to protect her from the ugly of what he'd done. Why couldn't he ever get it right with this girl?

Finally, she closed her eyes and pinched the bridge of her nose, letting out a long breath through tight lips. "I need to think."

As painful as it was to strip this down out in the open, he couldn't risk allowing her to walk away for two more years. She wiped a hand over her face and moved toward the door, and he stood, frozen in place, the weight of the last two years too heavy to let him stop her.

"No more secrets, Em. I promise."

She turned her eyes to him for a long moment and for a second, he thought she might come back, step back into his arms, and make his world right again. So he said the only thing that made sense, the desperate plea that his heart had made since she'd pulled in and he'd seen her father without the sling.

"I love you, Emma."

~

Emma closed her eyes and let her head drop back, the air coming out of her all at once at Noah's words.

The first time he'd said it, laying in his bed, looking so proud of himself, she'd known it was different than the last time, but right now, it felt exactly the same. Denver was happening; he was hurting and desperate. All the rational parts of her that knew he meant these words disappeared at the memory of him sitting slumped over in the passenger seat of her car, freedom so close she could taste it. Loving Noah *was* an abyss. It was easy to do. He was charming, familiar, and made her feel like she was the only girl in the world.

She wished he could have denied what happened with Layla, wished Jimmy had just been stirring up shit like he was known to do. She'd watched Noah transform before her eyes the year after Gavin died, but she'd never imagined he could get to the point he'd just confessed to. It was too much.

"Please don't," she begged, too late; the damage was done.

She opened her eyes and looked at him. In the place of the cool, calm, collected Noah she'd come to know since she'd come home from Denver was a desperate man.

She turned and went to the house without looking back.

THIRTY

NOAH PACED THE length of the Baylor's big kitchen in the dark, unable to stand still. Pausing, he looked out the kitchen window. He could see the back porch of the Pierce house from this vantage point, and when he caught himself hoping to see Emma come out the door, he pulled himself away, turning his back and crossing his arms. This wasn't healthy.

She'd said she needed to think, so he'd given her space overnight. That morning, he'd spotted Jonas heading out to the barn at first feed, so he hadn't bothered to go down, just in case he'd run into her. He had nothing to say to win her over, to excuse why he hadn't been up front about the way her absence had affected him, and then affected others.

Now the day was waning and at some point, her car had left and hadn't come back. He'd been busy bringing down heifers with Finn at midday and hadn't seen it leave, but a niggling panic was beginning to set in at the back of his brain. He'd told himself he would wait until she came and wanted to talk, but now he was beginning to think it was too late.

At first, he'd been furious that someone else had told her about Layla; though most of his mess had been very public, it was something he considered personal. Then he'd realized it didn't matter—it would have been ugly as hell no matter how it went down. He should have told her sooner, but there hadn't been a lull in their loving in which to fit that kind of conversation. It was just another in the long line of mistakes he'd made with Emma.

"You look like a storm cloud." Ren's soft voice emerged from the doorway. Dane and the kids were gone and the lights were off, he'd assumed she was gone with them. They'd come home from their honeymoon a week ago, refreshed and looking happier than ever, and her bump seemed to have grown considerably while they were gone.

"I didn't know you were here."

"I was taking a nap." She smiled softly and moved into the room, switching on a light. "This tapeworm takes a lot out of me."

"I hope I didn't wake you." Though he'd been here for a few months now, he still felt like he was an outsider looking in, sometimes.

She shook her head, laughing, and squeezed past him to get a glass from the cupboard and pour herself some water.

"You didn't, the tapeworm did. I have a

strong feeling this one's going to be a steer wrestler. Very athletic." Her happiness and warmth was contagious, and he found the stress in himself calming as she talked about his new niece or nephew. She leaned against the counter next to him, with her back turned to the window. "You look like you've got something on your mind."

He didn't want to talk. What he wanted to do was run down to the Pierce house, get on his knees, and beg Emma to give him one more chance he didn't deserve to get it right. He'd learned, however, that despite her quiet calm, there was never any sense in arguing with his sister-in-law. Once she'd become comfortable as a fixture in the household, she'd taken charge in a way that wasn't obtrusive or aggressive, but firm enough that you didn't try to pull one past her. She ran a house a lot like his mother had, and every last one of the Baylor boys, including Gage, listened when she spoke.

"Out with it," she insisted.

He rubbed a hand over his face and resisted the urge to look back out the window. "I'm too damn old for girl problems."

She laughed and shook her head. "We're a different creature altogether, Noah. No man is entirely immune to girl problems. Even your brother. Usually the problem is that we aren't communicating the way we ought to be."

After everything Dane and Ren had gone through to be together, he couldn't imagine the two of them weren't completely in tune with one another, but her face said otherwise. His older brother had the advantage of patience and quiet determination that he hadn't developed yet.

"You know what helps with that?" She cocked her head at him, her tone teasing.

"What?"

"Talking." She nodded encouragingly and patted him on the shoulder. "I don't really know Emma, but I've seen you two together and you look happier when you're with her than I've seen you since I came here."

He looked down at his feet, letting out a long breath. Not talking was what had gotten him here in the first place.

"Whatever it is, seems like it's worth the little walk down over the lawn to knock on her door and have a chat."

"You're probably right about that." He'd given her enough time. If they were serious about this moving forward, they needed to work this out now.

She looked at him expectantly. "So what are you waiting for?"

"Alright, alright." He laughed and gave Ren a gentle hug. He'd never anticipated when she'd rolled into town in that beat up GMC Jimmy that she'd eventually be the voice of reason for him. He pressed a kiss to her cheek and headed for the door.

Emma's car still wasn't in the yard at the Pierce's, so he decided to do a quick night check in the horse barn before he'd head down and wait her out. He slid the big door open, rehearsing what he'd say to Emma, and was surprised to hear an unfamiliar nicker. Alamo's head popped over the half door, ears perked, as Noah rounded the corner into the aisle. Frowning, four strides brought him to the horse. He rubbed the swirl in the middle of his forehead and plucked a handwritten note off the front of the stall. She had to have brought him while they were riding herd.

It was addressed to Kerri, but he opened it anyway.

Ker!
Sorry to have done this while you're at work, but they needed me in Denver right away. He's all yours. I'll come back in a couple of weeks to check on you, and if you need anything, call me.
Xoxo,
Emma

Resisting the urge to crush the note in his hand, he let out a long breath, refolded it and pinned it back on the door where he'd found it, for Kerri to find.

He walked out of the barn with resolve. It would have been easy to go back to the way he'd been after she left the first time, but there was no way he was talking himself into that bullshit excuse again. He'd said he'd follow her to the ends of the earth, and that was his intention.

THIRTY-ONE

"HEY." EMMA POKED her head in the tack room of Renegade's main barn and found Allison, the young groom from Canada, taking apart bridles to clean.

"Thank God." The younger girl jumped to her feet, looking thrilled to see her; then again, Allison was thrilled about just about anything. Her enthusiasm had gotten Emma through her fair share of homesickness. If she'd missed anything about Denver, it might have been Allison. Now she knew she'd take advantage of Allison's optimism to stop missing Noah.

Emma crushed her friend in a hug. Leaving on such short notice hadn't been fair and she could see the toll it had taken on Allison's face.

"I'm just gonna get changed and I'll come give you a hand."

"Hey, I've got today. You get settled in. But I do want you to look at Encore."

Emma nodded. The horse had come in a few weeks before her departure for rehabilitative treatment. Renegade Racing's high end clientele demanded things like their hyperbaric chamber and the pool for low impact muscle building.

Together, the girls walked the aisle to the end of the barn where their rehab horses were. Most of them were barrel racers dealing with strains and tears, nothing serious. Encore wasn't part of their string, but his owner, Lily Jacobs, was a friend of Banks' brother, Nate. He'd helped Lily connect with Emma, and Emma had used her tenure to convince her manager that Encore deserved a chance to recover at Renegade.

The tall black horse was standing in the back of his stall with his head in the corner. It was his normal stance, and she couldn't blame him. The horse's skin was a topography of scars, some from the accident, some from surgery to fix the things that had been damaged in the accident. He was lucky to be alive, and so was Lily.

"Hey, buddy." She spoke to him as she approached, putting a hand on his rump and working her way toward his head. Those scars had looked a lot worse until Emma had done some research on naturopathic treatments for them. "You been giving Ally trouble?"

Allison stood in the doorway and handed Emma a lead rope. She snapped it onto the horse's halter and led him out into the alley. Handing the rope to Allison, she watched as the girl led him up and down the aisle. He still had a pronounced limp, but she could see definite improvement in his muscle tone.

"You did fine, Ally." The girl's worried expression when she came back asked the question. "He *is* improving, you can see it right here." She pointed to the new muscle she saw.

"The vet has been saying really positive stuff."

"Has Lily been around?"

Allison nodded. Encore's owner had her own physical issues to work through after the horse and rider had been struck by a car legging up for distance riding. She'd been in a wheelchair the first time they'd met, and before Emma had left, she'd progressed on to crutches. The truth was in her eyes, though. There were parts of that kind of trauma that wouldn't heal with the physical wounds.

"You know, he just needs time." She stroked the horse's neck. "He might not ever be the same as he was, but he'll be okay."

Once she said the words, she realized they applied to more than just Encore. Noah had been through a lot, and now he was learning to be himself again, much like the horse. He'd hurt her, but he'd proven, over these months, that he wanted her—he wanted *them*. She could trust him without giving him the opportunity to hurt her, and the base of all that was communication. He'd wanted to talk, she should have let him.

As if on cue, her phone dinged in her pocket. She knew who it was; it had bleated out notifications of several calls and texts during the drive but she hadn't picked it up. All she knew for sure was that a little distance was supposed to clear her head, but now that she was here, she just wanted to get in her car and turn around.

Allison led Encore into the stall and unsnapped the lead rope. He went back to his position in the corner.

"You might as well go get settled. Now that I can quit being a nervous Nellie." Allison laughed.

"You did as good a job as I would have." Emma smiled, but her heart was down at the bottom of her belly, knowing she was going to have to face up to what she'd done soon enough. "Alright. I'm just going to go unload the car and then we'll go get dinner."

"Sounds good." Allison returned to her work as Emma strode out to the car, retrieving her duffle bag and backpack, then took the walkway along the outside of the barn back to what they called the 'bunkhouse'. It was a little bungalow not unlike Noah's house back in Three Rivers; one floor, a couple of bedrooms, and a shared space.

She closed herself in her bedroom, and pulled her cell phone out, with her nerves all tangled up at the bottom of her throat. She reminded herself that coming here had been self-preservation, but it sure didn't feel like it. She thumbed the screen to unlock the phone.

17:58 PM NOAH: EM.

She frowned, letting out a long breath. It crossed her mind to call instead of text, but her courage had flown out the window the second she'd gotten in her car this afternoon. She typed the only thing she could think to say.

18:10 PM EMMA: I'M SORRY.

18:12 PM NOAH: NONE OF THIS IS YOUR FAULT. YOU HAVE NOTHING TO BE SORRY FOR.

She held her phone between her hands and let out a long breath. She did, though. It hadn't been fair that he hadn't told her about Layla, but she hadn't given him a chance to, either. And she could have done something, anything, besides getting in her car and driving to Denver without sitting down to have a conversation with him. She'd been selfish. Her phone buzzed again.

18:15 PM NOAH: I BLINDSIDED YOU. THIS ISN'T OVER.

She swallowed back tears, but Lord knew she'd cried enough in the last twelve hours. Until her throat was raw and her eyes felt filled with sand. For Layla, and Gavin, and Sunny. And for Noah, and for herself. For her regret, and for her fear. And then she'd done the only thing she could think to do to get out of that cycle: she left.

This isn't over.

THIRTY-TWO

"ARE YOU ABSOLUTELY sure about this?" Noah squared Kerri up in his sights as the girl dismounted. "She left him for you to ride."

Kerri rolled her eyes and shook her head at him. "You really don't get it, do you?"

Sixteen year old girls? No, Noah didn't get those *at all*.

"You take the horse, you show up." She still held Alamo's reins as she used her hands to indicate his trajectory between Three Rivers and Denver. The minute she'd found out he was planning to go, she'd suggested he take Alamo. "She'll probably be happy to see you. And if she isn't, at least she'll be happy to see him."

"I wanted to give her some space." Now not only was he confused about teenage girls but also about *why* he would be trying to explain his relationship with Emma to a teenage girl.

Kerri let out an exasperated sigh and rolled

her eyes again. "Didn't you already do that once?"

"Yes," he said, a little too defensively.

"And how did that work out for you?" She put one hand on her hip and held Alamo's reins out to him.

"Look, I don't need any sass from you," he teased.

She gave him an exasperated look and pushed the reins at him again. "Take the horse."

He took the reins. "What about your season?"

She shrugged. "My season will be fine. Besides, Buckshot's still got things to teach me. And that filly you brought up from Reicher will be ready soon enough."

He watched her as she turned, ending the conversation, and headed for the house. She was a softer soul than she was portraying right now, so he knew she'd be hurting a little bit, and he added her to his growing list of amends to make. So far, it included Dane, Finn, his parents, and Jonas, with Emma right at the top. Underlined twice.

It was as good a plan as any. The alternative was the bottom of a fifth of vodka and a ditch along the highway. Their texts the night before hadn't been satisfying, but it had been something that said she was still open to this. She'd surprised him by calling later on in the evening. The sound of her voice was a relief, but it wasn't the same as being able to hold her, touch her, feel the pulse under her skin. Truth was, even if she hadn't left the way she had, he couldn't imagine a world where he could have dealt with the distance between them anymore.

She hadn't asked him to come, but she also hadn't outright said not to. And there was hurt in her voice that he could only soothe in person. It meant unsaid words. He'd let her go without following once. There had been enough mistakes in the last two years that he knew this was one he couldn't make twice. If this was what it took, he would do it ten times over.

He'd gone into town and picked up a few things that morning, stopped to chat with Jonas and Myrna, and called ahead to Nate Montgomery to make sure he had room for him to crash with the horses for a while.

"Alright, buddy. I guess we're going on a road trip." He patted the gelding's neck lightly and headed for the barn to strip his tack.

Finn met him in the door of the barn. "Dane says you're going to Denver."

Noah nodded, slipped Alamo into his stall, and re-emerged, closing the door behind him. He still had a few other things to pack up, but they'd be ready to roll within an hour. He expected Finn to be angry, but his brother's face was soft and he grasped Noah's shoulder.

"*Finally,* you're doing something that makes sense."

It meant a lot coming from Finn, who had told him more than once in the last few years that he'd been doing the *wrong* thing. He nodded.

"I was stupid once to let her stay gone. If I

do it again, I'm just an asshole."

Finn grinned. "You said it, not me."

~

Emma bustled out of the tack room with an armload of tangled leg wraps fresh from laundry. The bright sun called to her and she knew she'd feel a little more human if she did some of her work outside instead of inside the cool barn. She heard an engine in the yard, but thought nothing of it, pausing to peek into one of the stalls as she passed by. When she looked up again, she spotted a silhouette standing in the big square of sunlight from the double doors. A figure all too familiar. Her heart and her steps quickened. Those dusty Justin boots and the stupid ballcap. Without realizing it, she dropped the leg wraps and he stepped inside the door of the barn when he saw her.

She let out an anxious breath, her stomach full of nerves and paused for a second before she stepped closer, winding her arms around his neck.

He couldn't have been expecting her response because it took a second, but then he tightened his arms around her and she felt his hand drift up her back, to the base of her neck, tipping her head back. Noah's eyes were filled with emotion, the same she felt rising up. It wouldn't have bothered her if the entire Renegade team was watching them right now, her heart and her mind could only think about the fact that he was *here* and in his arms felt like the most natural place to be.

He spoke first, his words coming quickly and full of emotion. "I should have been honest with you, right from the start. And that goes back years. The summer Gavin died, I think I was starting to realize what I wanted. But you get scared, and then you get hurt, and then you get stupid. At least that's the order it happened in for me. I've got a whole hell of a lot to make up to you, and if you want to know about every stupid thing I did after you left, I'll tell you everything." He grimaced. "It's not pretty, and if it weren't for Finn, it would have ended in a twisted up car wreck."

She let out a breath she didn't know she'd been holding, her heart full to bursting. She hadn't intended to make him follow her, but she was glad he had. It meant he *had* grown, he *was* different. Noah from two years ago would have hunkered down in Three Rivers and hurt.

"I love you," she responded.

Even though she wasn't sure he felt it, he put that casual, tipped up smile onto his lips.

"We had to both come all the way to Denver for you to say that?" Despite his teasing tone, she felt him tighten his hold on her. He ducked his head and brushed his lips across her with the lightest of touches and electricity ran through her.

"I love you too, Em. And there isn't a thing in the world that's going to stop me from doing that anymore."

"I'm sorry. I should have trusted you. I should have let us talk when you wanted to. I thought coming back here might help me clear my head. I didn't mean for you to have to chase me down."

"Doesn't matter." He shook his head. "We're here to be with you."

"*We*?"

He gestured behind him to his rig – the truck and a two horse trailer and her heart skipped a couple of beats.

"You didn't..." The only thing nearly as good as him being right here, touching her, was what, or *who* might be in that trailer.

"I did."

"What about Kerri?"

He laughed, turned her and tucked her under his arm as they headed toward the trailer.

"It was her idea, actually."

He pulled the man door open and both Alamo and Blackjack dropped their heads to look out, their ears pricked, looking for treats. They'd traveled together for eons and this was their standard routine, though Noah always admonished her for giving them treats at every stop.

"And 'Jack?"

"Yeah. Not for you. For me."

Her heart and her mind weren't communicating properly, because she couldn't wrap her head around why he'd be here with both horses, and...the bed of his truck had a suitcase in it. Sweet Jesus.

"But you love Three Rivers..."

"I love *you* more. I'll find work, you'll finish

out your contract, and then we'll go home. Or somewhere else. Or stay right here. I'd follow you to the ends of the earth, Em, if it meant that I got to call you mine forever."

Forever. That was a big word. She swallowed hard when she felt him take her hand and slide a ring onto her finger. Her heart raced like a stampede of wild horses, her stomach twisted into knots before she finally looked down at her left hand. The ring was simple—a white gold band with a few channel set diamonds—no muss, no fuss. And exactly what she would have picked for herself.

"This is where I'm supposed to be. Wherever you are." He spoke while she stared at the ring, too stunned to respond. "I can't promise I won't mess up, but I *can* promise that I will wake up every morning doing the best I can to be exactly the man that someone like you deserves, Em. You're every good thing that I've never been, all the softness, and kindness, and patience that I've never been able to accomplish. And I want that, every single day.

"Will you be my wife, Emma Pierce? You're already practically a Baylor. Let's make it official."

She lifted her eyes to his; his expression was earnest and a smile played over his lips. Tears welled up in her eyes and she took him in. There had never been a time when she'd ever expected *not* to spend the rest of her life with Noah in it; it had just never crossed her mind that it would be like *this*. She had never been able to wrap her head around what world would exist where someone like him would want someone like her. *This world. It's this one,* she reminded herself.

When she didn't reply right away, he continued, his words hurried. "I meant to do that proper. On one knee. After a fancy dinner. But I got too damn excited when you came running into my arms."

He tugged her to him and pressed a kiss to her forehead, then the end of her nose, and then he took her mouth with a kiss that was long and full of wanting. A culmination of two days apart made her wonder how they'd ever spent two *years* away from one another. When he pulled away, he rested his forehead against hers, cinched his arms around her waist tight, and laughed low.

"Say yes, Emma."

She cupped his jaw in her hand and drew in a breath. They had a long way to go, but she could commit to this. She could commit to him. Because it didn't matter whether there was a ring on her finger or not, she knew that if they were parted, they would find one another again and again.

Alamo took that opportunity to let out a throaty nicker, as if he was backing Noah up and Emma laughed out loud.

"Yes!"

EPILOGUE

"CLOSE YOUR EYES," Noah said, looking over at Emma. They'd just turned off the main drag and were heading toward the ranches. She was slouched down in the passenger seat of his truck with their new puppy, Tucker, cradled in her arms. He was fast approaching way-too-big-for-lapdog status, but neither of them minded. Noah chided her about it all the time. The merle pup was sound asleep.

She rolled her eyes at him. "Noah, it's home."

"I know, but you haven't been here in a while. I just want you to see it with fresh eyes."

A little smile quirked the corner of his lips. She recognized that look; she'd seen it enough in the last few months. He was up to something. He'd developed a healthy appetite for pleasant surprises as her fiancé and the ring had been just the start.

"Just humor me for a minute."

She rolled her eyes again but when he put

his blinker on like he was going to pull the whole rig over and stop if she didn't comply, she closed them. Her stomach fluttered with the same butterflies it got every time they'd come home for a weekend since he'd come to Denver. They hadn't been home in two months, not since little Grace had been born. They were both completely smitten with his new niece, but they'd been busy and managed to get by on pictures Kerri texted them every day.

"Thank you." She heard him say. Tucker shifted in his sleep and she put a hand on his belly.

Being away from home with him made her want Three Rivers more than ever, and it hadn't taken long for her to decide they'd go back as soon as she was released from her contract.

The last eight months had been a little bit of everything she hadn't expected. He'd been right when he'd said it wasn't over. He and the horses had put up at Nate Montgomery's place, which was about ten miles down the road from Renegade and they'd assumed the closest thing to a normal courtship they'd be capable of.

She slept in the bunkhouse through the week and spent weekends in the little apartment above the barn at Nate's with Noah. Alamo was back in shape and she'd even hit a couple of the local jackpots with some success. They'd come home a handful of times, but in the end, they had agreed that being together in a place they weren't so comfortable in helped them grow their relationship in ways that were necessary.

The process of unraveling the year after

she'd left had been long, painful, and not without tears, but they'd holed up in his apartment from the first Friday afternoon he was there until the following Monday morning so they could work it all out, with the promise that neither would leave until it was over, no matter how painful it was. Knowing his vulnerabilities opened a whole other side of Noah up to her, and made her love him more.

A mile up the road, he turned left—the Baylor driveway...but instead of the half mile up to the house, he turned right, and stopped. Her brow furrowed and she squeezed her eyes shut tighter to resist the urge to peek. He turned the engine off.

"Keep them closed," she heard him speak as the truck shifted and he got out. Tucker wiggled out of her arms and followed him out the driver's side door and in a second, she heard him opening the passenger's side door. He put his hand on her arm and helped her out, guiding her over gravel. She giggled.

"Come on, this is silly."

"Open up."

When she opened her eyes, she was standing in front of a little log house. A couple of acres had been cleared on the property lines at the front of the Baylor and Pierce spreads. A rough lean-to barn and small corral had been assembled behind the small house.

She looked from the house to Noah, and back again.

"I don't understand."

"It's ours."

When she could only look at him dumbfounded, he laughed and reached for her hand, pulling her a bit closer.

"I know it's a bit premature, but can I carry you across the threshold, Future-Mrs.-Baylor?"

"You can't..." She raised a brow, but before she could protest a second more, he'd scooped her up into his arms like it was no effort at all. A trill of laughter burst out of her and she wound her arms around his neck to steady herself.

"Oh but I can." He grinned, pressing a kiss to her cheek and navigating their bodies carefully up the stairs and into the cabin.

She kicked her feet and he let her down to explore. It was small, but more spacious than his apartment at Nate's. An open floor housed an eat-in kitchen and small living room, with a bedroom and bathroom off to the left. A big window looked out over the corral in the back.

"You didn't think I was going to let you move back in with your mama and daddy when we came back, did you? We've been sleeping apart long enough."

She laughed as he pulled her body to his, Tucker dancing around their feet, wiggling and whining. He pressed his lips to the column of her neck just under her jaw, his breath warm on her skin. "It's not much."

Swallowing, she pressed a hand to her throat, overwhelmed by the idea of them having their own little space, so close to their families.

"Noah Baylor, you know I'd live in a tin can

with you, right? But what about *your* house?"

He loosened his grip on her and shrugged nonchalantly. "I put it on the market the day I came to Denver. It sold a couple of months ago, and that's when I started to put this together."

Her brows shot up. "You sold it."

Nodding, he squeezed her waist lightly. "I sold it so I could do this. Everybody helped...your daddy, Cutter, Finn and Dane. It's a little rough yet...but it's *ours*. A place for us to be us again, without the tough memories around every corner."

"It's perfect," she sighed. "It's home."

HOMECOMING HEART

ABOUT THE AUTHOR

Amity Lassiter lives in Eastern Canada with her herding dog, her barn cat, two horses and her Mister. She has loved telling stories her entire life and even before she could write could be found in her grandmother's basement, reciting fiction into an ancient cassette recorder.

The most influential author in Amity's life would be Peter S. Beagle, the author of The Last Unicorn, who introduced her to her first achingly impossible love story and made her believe in magic. She met, and shared the most surreal small talk with Beagle in May 2014.

She loves critters, coffee, and cowboys—and she still believes in unicorns.

You can find more from Amity Lassiter online at www.amitylassiter.com